Ben's Binoculars:

Journey of the Ruby-Throat

T.W. MAHN

This book is a work of fiction. Any resemblance to actual events or persons, living or dead, is entirely coincidental.

"Ben's Binoculars: Journey of the Ruby-Throat," by T.W. Mahn. ISBN 978-1-62137-609-5 (Softcover).

Published 2014 by Virtualbookworm.com Publishing Inc., P.O. Box 9949, College Station, TX 77842, US. ©2014, T.W. Mahn. All rights reserved. No part of this publication may be reproduced, stored in a retrieval system, or transmitted in any form or by any means, electronic, mechanical, recording or otherwise, without the prior written permission of T.W. Mahn.

Special thanks to:

Robert Sargent of the Hummer Bird Study Group and Dr. John Dindo of the Dauphin Island Sea Lab for their helpful discussion and reviews of the information contained in this book. Thanks also to Landa Ellsworth and Audrey Phillips for their beneficial feedback of the manuscript.

Ben's Binoculars:

Journey of the Ruby-Throat

Contents

I. Vacation 1

II. Seabird Island 7

III. The House on The Bay 12

IV. The Gift 20

V. Birding 26

VI. A World I Never Knew Existed 34

VII. Some Answers to My Questions 40

VIII Migration South 48

IX. On to Mexico and Discovery 64

X. On the Shore 70

XI. Chichen Itza 86

XII. On to the Unknown 100

XIII. Costa Rica 110

XIV. Return Home 124

XV. The Key 136

Epilogue: What I Learned After the Trip 144

Bibliography 150

For Angie, Elijah, and Matthew

I. Vacation

I'm not sure why all of this happened to a boy like me, but I'm glad that it did, and my life will never be the same. To people who know me I'm just Ben, but my full name is Benjamin William Armstrong. My family and I have lived in Mountain Home, Arkansas for as long as I can remember. It's a beautiful place, with small mountains nearby, lakes and streams, and the people are pretty nice. But I've always been restless, wanting to travel all over the world. Kids in my fifth grade class pick on me at school because I love to spend time in the library reading about other places whenever I finish my work in the classroom. My teacher lets me go there and read to my heart's content, or go online in the computer lab if I have enough classroom points. But I don't care if they tease me, I love to learn.

It all started on Mom's birthday when she got a really nice set of binoculars and a bird watching book. Dad got them for her, knowing how she loves birds. She has the most wonderful garden specifically designed for different kinds of birds. She watches the birds as they migrate every year past our house, south in the fall of the year, and north in the spring. I was happy for her, as she likes that sort of thing. Soon after that, Dad got some binoculars as well, and they would sit out on the porch swing for hours looking at birds and finding them in the book together. Sometimes my little sister Beth and I would sit out there with them, but usually by the time they spotted one and passed the binoculars to us, the bird had moved on and we didn't get to see it. This all seemed rather boring to us, so we would go inside and read or build things on our own, or go exploring in the woods, pretending we were traveling to far off places.

Once a year, my family travels down to an island along the northern coast of the Gulf of Mexico and spends time with different aunts, uncles, and cousins, but most of all Grandpa and Grandma! We go fishing, watch the birds, collect shells, eat fish, shrimp, and thoroughly enjoy ourselves. These are the only trips of any distance I have ever really been on, unless you count school field trips to Little Rock, and those make me even more restless. I wanted to travel, *really* travel, by ship, airplane, train, submarine, even into outer space someday, and every program I had ever watched about being an astronaut, or pilot, or anything of significance said that I should work hard in school. So I did.

We made the trip to the island in the fall, when the first crisp October mornings began to turn the maples golden and fiery red. It coincided with our fall break at school, and the teachers always assigned homework during that week. I tried to get ahead on my schoolwork before I went, and usually had to bring some work with me to do. I wished we could travel in the summer like other families, but it was cheaper to go in the fall, and the beaches we went to were much less crowded, so the shelling was better. Besides, Mom said that October was "the best time to be down on the island." The temperature was always in the 80s, and we could swim in the water when the pools back home had all closed down for winter. Mom made me do all of my homework the first day, so I could enjoy the rest of the time with more freedom.

The house on the island was nothing special to look at with its weather-worn cedar boards on the outside, although it had plenty of space inside. When I was younger, I thought it was really cool because it was built on stilts so high that you could drive cars under it. This building method was used with most of the houses near the water, and it was always great to see those houses up on stilts. It was one and a half stories with a single large room on the main level that served as the kitchen, dining room, and living room all rolled into one, and a couple of bedrooms down a hallway that led to a year-round porch.

I always thought that the back porch was something really special because it had removable windows that made it a screened in porch for most of the year, but then became a fully enclosed sun room during the winter months. There was a central staircase in the main room that led up to a small room on either side of the landing at the top of the stairs with a little bathroom between them. That was always where the kids stayed when we came. Grandma and Grandpa had bought it years ago so that Grandpa would have a place to go and fish, and Grandma would go into one of the small roof-angled upstairs rooms to see the sunlight on the water and paint pictures of the scenery before the porch was built. They had worked hard through the years to keep it. Now they spent several months of their retirement there each year, but the rest of the time it was rented out to other people who liked to be near the beach.

This trip, I decided that rather than watching the same videos in the car for the forty-second time, I would go ahead and do my homework so that I would have more time to play and explore when I got there. The only problem was I kept nodding off and would wake up 46 miles later. After fighting sleep for about 100 miles, I gave in and slept for a while and then got back to my homework. By the time we arrived at Seabird Island, I had done most of it, and only had to work at the house for about 30 minutes. It was a good excuse to get some time to myself. This was good because it was always a bit overwhelming arriving at the house. We came every year, and different Aunts and Uncles' families came each year, so we always saw different people from my extended family.

This year my Dad's brother's family would be here. Uncle Bob and Aunt Rachel were nice enough, but their only son Ned was a spoiled, immature jerk, so I was glad to have an excuse to go to my room, unpack, and get all of my homework done so I could be free the rest of the week. As I walked into the small upstairs room that had always been mine, I was surprised to see the normal double bed that I had had to myself as long as I could remember replaced with bunk beds. There was a desk in the corner, so I did my work, and unpacked my stuff into the small wicker chest of drawers in the room. I got out my pocket knife which I had recently earned in Scouts and slipped it into my pocket. After all of the work that I did earning the right to carry it, I was determined to look for uses here where I was allowed to have it. It would be great to have my own knife on fishing trips!

No sooner had I unpacked than Ned showed up and proclaimed that he had top bunk. "What?" I said surprised as I turned around to see his wild hair and freckly face, and he told me that we got to stay in the same room together this year. "Isn't that cool?" he said. I really didn't think that was cool, because he liked to be as annoying as possible, always in your face, and we didn't like the same things *at all*. I smiled at him and went downstairs.

Ned was the last person I wanted to spend my time with on this trip. He was only a year younger than me, but he acted like he was in kindergarten sometimes, and did whatever he could to get my attention, being as rude as possible. Last fall, I had spent several hours perfecting a big sand castle on the South Beach with shells supporting the arches and a large moat around it. I was just getting ready to fill the moat with water when I heard a belching sound behind me. No sooner had I turned to see who it was than Ned came scuffing up with a super soaker and doused me with ice cold water before letting loose on my sand castle, destroying most of it. He had the whole beach to play on! Why did he have to come and ruin my hours of work? There was no way I was going to have him sleeping in my room, putting frogs in my bed or who knows what else. I went downstairs to talk to Dad.

"Dad, can I talk to you for a minute?" I said. He could tell I was irritated.

"What is it, Son?" he asked. I told him and he then told me that Uncle Bob had just suggested the idea to him, and that he thought it was a good idea.

"And you never thought to ask *me*?" I said.

"We really didn't think you would mind. He *is* your cousin, and besides, it's only for a week. I think it will be good for both of you," Dad said.

Good for both of us. Hah! The last time I did something with Ned, a bunch of us were fishing and he thought it was hilarious to run from one side of the boat to the other until it almost tipped over, miles out in the Gulf. I was sick for hours, hurling over the side, and the adults didn't do anything.

"Do you remember the fishing incident, and the sand castle?" I asked.

"That was a year ago. You're still not sore about that, are you?" Dad said. "Besides, he is a year older now. He's almost as tall as you are."

"Maybe so, but that doesn't mean he has grown up any," I said.

"Then maybe it's time *you* should," Dad said seriously looking me straight in the eyes, and he turned and went outside, down the steps to the car.

II. Seabird Island

I was devastated. Here I had been looking forward to the only trip we would take this year, and now I had to spend it in a room with *Ned*. That would mean that the only alone time I would get on this trip I had just spent—doing homework. Icck! I decided to go for a walk by myself, and as I walked down the street, Grandpa and Grandma drove up. I ran back to the house to see them, and immediately asked if I could help them unload their car. It was always good to see Grandpa and Grandma. They got out, all smiles and gave hugs and kisses all around, and my parents and the rest of the clan came out to greet them. After helping them, I forgot about my walk and went back to my room.

Ned had put up posters of strange bands on the walls, and was sitting in the corner listening to his ipod so loud that I could hear it from the hallway. I told him he would lose his hearing doing that, and he just shouted, "What?!" I just shook my head and went over to the desk and put my books away. "You brought homework to the island? I didn't know you were that much of a nerd. I can't believe I've got to spend this week with a dweeb." Ned said.

"I thought I was your favorite cousin," I said.

"You were, before I remembered how much of a dweeb you are," he retorted.

I hadn't thought of it that way before. Ned and I didn't see eye to eye, but I had just been thinking about how I didn't want to be with him, not about whether or not he wanted to stay with me this week. I decided to try to make the best of it.

"Whatcha' listenin' to?" I asked.

"It's this new band, you'll love it. Take a listen," Ned said.

I didn't love it, but he got out the lyrics sheet and showed it to me, and surprisingly, the lyrics were kind of poetic, in a punky-funky sort of way. It grew on me once I knew the words. Maybe this was the kind of growing up Dad was talking about, actually trying to understand Ned a little more.

It wasn't long before the dinner bell rang. My little sister Beth, being the youngest, got to ring it. The bell had been on an old ship that had been mothballed in the bay, and when it was retired, the bells on it were retired as well. My Grandpa had gotten the bell because he had helped the captain of the ship one time in a storm, and the captain told him that when the ship was eventually retired, he could have one thing on it. He chose the brass bell. Every year, the youngest of the kids here that week would get the job of polishing the bell and ringing it at meal times.

The first family meal on the island was always Seafood. We would stop at a fish market and pick up some fish that had been caught that day off of the boat. Each family would pick up something different, and we would have quite a feast! Fresh

Grouper, Flounder, Red Snapper, and whatever else they happened to catch was on the menu. And of course, there was the shrimp! They would almost melt in your mouth if you just peeled them and cooked them up in a little butter. Ned had talked Uncle Bob into buying some calamari and placing them cold and raw in the middle of the table, little squid standing up on toothpicks with their tentacles sticking out everywhere and eyes looking right at us.

I decided to eat out on the screened-in porch to be as far as possible from those protruding eyes staring at me. It wasn't long before all three of us kids were out there, and Grandpa came out to tell us stories. The whole family went for a walk on the beach to watch the sunset, and then as the stars came out one by one, we came back to the house and Grandpa told more stories on the screened-in porch.

Ned requested one I didn't remember hearing before about an old house on the island. Grandpa began, "About 300 years ago, when this island was owned by the French, before the Fort was built to keep war ships out of the bay, there were Native People here. The Natives and the French got along for the most part, but each had practices that were strange to the other, and they kept their distance.

One day, a French soldier had just completed his duties and was fishing in the surf for some dinner when he heard a woman crying out as if in severe distress. He reeled in, set his pole upright in the sand, and took off toward the sound. A group of young men were harassing the young

Native woman, and she was terrified, unable to understand their language. She was shouting at them in her own language, but they just kept coming. He ran to the group telling them to leave her alone, and they began to surround him. The soldier drew out a pistol, and the men backed off, one by one. The woman came and bowed to him, thanking him for helping her, and as she looked up at him, he noticed in her eyes a depth and kindness he had never seen in any woman's eyes before. This intrigued him to the point that he couldn't get her out of his mind for a long time. He vowed to learn her language, and after many years, they overcame their differences and married.

The soldier had a small house built for them to live in, and from then on relations between the French and the Natives improved on the Island. It was a good time. After many years, political times had changed, and the French were getting pressured from the Mother Country to take over the island completely for themselves, removing the Natives."

"Grandpa," I said, "What is the Mother Country?" Ned snickered at me, although I don't know why. I was sure he didn't know what it was.

"I don't suppose you have gotten to that term yet in school, so that is a good question," he said. Ned stopped his snickering immediately as Grandpa said, "The Mother Country for this land was at that time—France."

Grandpa went on. "The soldier's wife was spared the relocation, and she begged unsuccessfully for her people to be allowed to stay. As the Natives left, the chief gave her a gift that no one understands to this day. It is said that years later when her beloved husband died at a ripe old age, she mourned for him and then used the gift to travel on the wings of the birds to her people. The house still stands today, although it is in severe disrepair."

"It's that *haunted* place on the East End of the island on the bay near the fort, isn't it?" Ned said.

"That is the house. But if it's haunted, it's only with good magic, for there was never anything but love there," Grandpa replied.

"I don't think so. I think her sadness haunts the place," Ned said.

III. The House on The Bay

The next day Dad said that we were all going bird watching in the afternoon. I was thinking that it would be just like at home, with no binoculars for me to see the birds. So after breakfast, I finally got my chance to go for a walk by myself.

"Hold up a minute!" shouted Ned from the steps of the house once I had gotten about half way to the beach. I wanted to sneak behind a palm tree and hide, but instead I turned and said, "What is it?"

"I want to come, too." Ned said.

"I'm just going for a walk along the beach, *alone*. I don't even know how far I'm going," I replied.

A gleam came into Ned's eye briefly as he caught up to me, but he said nothing more. We walked along, picked up shells, and we played with a great big horseshoe crab for a while, all the time walking further and further East. We got to the point where we could see the old Civil War Fort, and Ned said, "Let's go to the house on the Bay. You know, the *haunted* one."

I was having none of it.

"I don't believe in haunted houses, and I don't want to go there," I said.

"What's the matter, you *scared*?" Ned asked.

"No. I just don't want to go there," I said.

"If you don't believe in haunted houses, then there's nothing to be afraid of, is there?" Ned said.

"Okay, then. Let's go," I said. He would badger me to death if we didn't go. I checked my watch and noted that it was only about ten in the morning. We had plenty of time to gawk at this place and still get back to our house for lunch and bird watching this afternoon. We turned off the beach onto the old boardwalk and went over the bridge of a little salt inlet before arriving in front of a quaint old Colonial style house. It was a bit dilapidated, there were boards missing in the upper attic area, and it really *did* look haunted.

"Last one in is a rotten egg!" shouted Ned as he began to break into a run. I knew we could get into trouble if we went in, so I didn't want to go. Just at that moment, I heard a car horn sound behind us, and was sure we were caught by the police. Surprisingly, it was Grandpa in his car.

"I was wonderin' where you boys had got to, and had a feelin' after that story last night that you might come here," Grandpa said through his car window. He stopped the car, got out, and ambled over to us.

"This is the place...lots of history here. Oh, if only the walls of this place could talk. What a story they could tell!" Grandpa said in an almost wonder.

"Is this house really as old as all that?" I said.

"This house has been added to and added to, although you wouldn't know it from out here," Grandpa said.

"You mean you've been *inside*!" Ned and I said, almost together.

"Yup. Years ago I knew a man who wanted to fix up the place. Said it was in his family's heritage. British guy from the Lake District in England," Grandpa said.

"I thought you told us last night that this place was built by a Frenchman," I said.

"So I did. But, you see, as time went on, the English took the island over for a brief time. Most of it reverted back to the French. Then, the Americans got it as part of the Louisiana Purchase. Don't they teach you about this stuff in school?" Grandpa said.

"Yes, they do. But it's in books and stuff. It's a lot different when you are standing on the same sand as all of those people before," I said.

"So it is, so it is, my boys. Well, let's walk around the place. It's living history, it is," Grandpa said, and began walking around the house, gazing upwards at its eaves.

We noticed that when we walked around the back, the screen door was open, banging in the gentle ocean breeze. The back door stood ajar just slightly, and one could see in just enough to tell that it was a kitchen. Grandpa walked up to the door to shut it when the door opened suddenly, and out popped the small head of a man who spoke with a British accent, "Whatcha' doin' here, you lot?"

We were too stunned to move. Only Grandpa chuckled.

"Is that you, Graham?" asked Grandpa.

"It is, and who are—", and with a sudden recognition he said, "Well, bless me! Old Ichabod! I never thought I'd see ye again! How have ye been, and who have ye brought wi' ye?"

I had forgotten that Grandpa's name was Ichabod. No one in my family ever called him anything but Grandpa, even his own children.

"These are two of my grandchildren. I have three more, but they aren't here this week," Grandpa laughed as he spoke. "How have you been?"

"Fine. Fine. I jes' come here to check up on a few things every now and again," Graham said.

"So, your name is Graham and you live in this old, rundown place, then?" Ned asked as rudely as ever. I was still too stunned to speak.

"Eh? Yeah, that's my name and this is my place. But everyone around here just calls me 'Ol' Salt'. It's easier on them." Ol' Salt said.

"I like that name, Ol' Salt. I mean, it sort of…well, it fits you." I said. I was still as nervous as could be.

Ol' Salt was an interesting old gentleman. Of slight build, he was very spry, energetic, and seemed a bit nervous for his age. His movements were strangely bird like, moving from one place to another in a sort of hopping maneuver, and he moved his head from side to side in a constant motion. His bright blue-silver eyes fixed on points even while the rest of his body continued to sway, and you felt as if he was staring right through you when he looked your way. He looked both of us over with those piercing eyes.

"Two fine lads, I mus' say," said Ol' Salt with a toothy smile. "But where are my manners? Come in, come in. It's good to have company."

We entered the house and saw clutter everywhere: old things, discarded things put neatly into trash cans but never taken out, and many maps from all over the world. I love maps, and couldn't help myself. Cautiously, I walked over to a wall in the next room with a large map of North and South America with all kinds of arrows drawn in different colors, and individual places marked as if they were something extra special. The arrows went all over, from up into Alaska, Canada, and Greenland in the northern part, and down to Chile and Argentina in the southern part. Slowly and carefully, I approached the Map. Ned was looking at some old junk in the corner, and Grandpa was talking to Ol' Salt. I quickly lost track of both of them as I became lost in the journeys this Map represented.

"Like maps, do ya'?" I heard Ol' Salt say excitedly from behind me.

"Yes, sir," I said tentatively. "I study them whenever I get the chance. But I've never seen any like these before."

"Nor will you see any like 'em again, I'll warrant," said Ol' Salt. "Made these myself. The ones you buy in the store are not nearly accurate enough, and they don't include the important things, like where to find the right food and stuff."

I stared at him. "Find the *right* food?" I said. "What kind of food is the right food?"

"Whatever kind I've got a hankerin' for," he laughed, and slapped his knee. Something was not right with this guy.

"What do these purple lines mean?" I asked, changing the subject. I pointed to a line on the map that stretched northward through the middle of the United States into Canada, and then west toward Barrow, Alaska, with dots on it all along the way. Then, it had one big dot right on Seabird Island, and another line leading southward along Mexico and Central America, leading all the way down to Argentina, again with dots all along the route as if someone were marking a trip they had taken.

"Ah, but you're a curious one, you are. I like that in a boy. I was curious as could be when I was your age. What are you, about nine?"

"Ten, sir," I said.

"That's even better. I was a curious ten-year old myself when I first began—" and he broke off. "But you seem a bit more cautious than I was. That could be a very good thing." This last remark was made more to himself than to me. "Those lines are the migration patterns for the White-Rumped Sandpiper."

Suddenly an obnoxious laughter broke through the room. Ned thought that was the funniest thing he had ever heard. He came over guffawing, and said, "The *what* kind of rump *who* piper? Come on, let's go. This guy's a loon in a broken down old house with a bunch of junk!"

"I am *not* a loon! I am many things, but have *never* been a loon!" Ol' Salt said, staring fixedly at Ned, suddenly very serious. For a split second I was worried he might do something to Ned for that seemingly innocuous comment, although I'm not sure what the old man could have done.

I eyed the Map more closely, and saw that there were hundreds of lines, all slightly different colors or with dotted lines, dashed lines, all with dots on them as if they marked stops along the way. Some had stops very often, and others had long stretches with no stops.

"I get it!" I blurted out. "These are all different types of birds, and the routes they take when they migrate."

"Aye, that they are," Ol' Salt said. "You are a bright young lad."

"But how did *you* find out about them in this kind of detail?" I asked.

"Let's just say I have devoted me life to learnin' as much about them as I can, and leave it at that," Ol' Salt said. "Ah, but I have lived a full life, and am just here goin' through some things to see what can be saved, and thinkin' how wonderful it would be to have someone to pass some of this stuff on to."

He turned to Grandpa as if something had just occurred to him. "Ichabod," he said, "I'm gettin' old and have got no children or grandchildren that I can give things to, and I have long lost track of my brothers and sisters and nephews and nieces. Would you mind if I share some things with your grandchildren?"

"You'll have to ask them," Grandpa said, turning to us both.

"You bet!" Ned said, and walked quickly over between Ol' Salt and me. "I want to have *that*." He pointed to an old barometer that would indicate weather, temperature, time and tide clock. It looked as if it had come out of an old ship. That was typical Ned. One minute, he was insulting the man's junk and the next he couldn't live without it.

"Help yourself, me laddie," Ol' Salt said.

"What about ye, me boy? What do ye think ye could use from Ol' Salt?" he asked with a twinkle in his eye.

I couldn't think of anything but going bird watching that afternoon with my family and having no binoculars. So I said, "Sir, I really could use some binoculars."

He grinned a large, knowing grin, and bent down like a Great Heron moving its head towards the water. "Are you sure that's all you want from Ol' Salt?" He asked.

"I think so, but these maps are amazing. I don't suppose I could take a picture of them?"

"Sure, sure!" he laughed. "Take all the pictures ye like! Ye may find that they come in handy one day." And he disappeared down some stairs into a sort of concreted out basement-like structure.

"That was the old ice box," Grandpa said. "They used to keep everything cold down there before refrigeration." I waited for Ol' Salt's return as Ned looked over his "new" weather station and tide chart. He was thrilled.

IV. The Gift

It wasn't long before Ol' Salt returned with a grin from ear to ear like a parrot with its mouth half open. In his hands was something he had obviously treasured, although its appearance looked beaten up, almost to the point of ruin. It was a very old hard leather bag with a heavy leather strap in the rough shape of a binocular case, with the initials *GAK* emblazoned on the side. He opened the case with some bravado, as if he was about to see something he loved for the last time.

"Come on, already. Let's see it!" a voice from behind me said as I gazed fixedly at the cloth wrapping he removed from within the case. Ned was being annoyingly impatient again. He ignored Ned and carefully removed the contents of the case. They were wrapped in an old rag that I was sure had once been white, but now was yellow and tattered. As he unwrapped the rag, he revealed a pair of brass Binoculars.

"There are some important things to remember when using *these* binoculars, boy," Ol' Salt said. "You've got to look through *both of these, like so*." He held them up to his eyes like a normal pair of binoculars. "And then you've got to line this middle line up with the bird you are looking at, and then you've got to—" his voice trailed off as if he were unable to share the last part of his wisdom, like he was worried about getting carried away and saying something he shouldn't.

"Yes, yes, and then you adjust the focus and see the bird. We've got it, old man," Ned said, not even noticing that he had interrupted an awkward silence. Nobody likes a know-it-all, and Ol' Salt gave him a look of irritation as if he wanted to say more, but became tight lipped and gave no more instructions. Slowly, he handed me the Binoculars.

Since Ned had brought this to my attention, I noticed that there wasn't any focus adjustment, and decided to ask Ol' Salt about it. He said that I wouldn't have to worry about it much, as he never had to in all the years he had used them. "But remember this well," he said, looking at all of us like a man choosing his words carefully, and then honing his gaze on me as if I was the only thing in the whole world that mattered to him in that very moment. "If used properly and for good, these will change your life for the better. Life isn't always easy, but it's the toughest parts that make you stronger. Mark these words well." I thought this a strange thing to say when passing on a pair of binoculars, but nodded my head anyway. I looked down at this new gift that was now in my hands.

The Binoculars themselves were peculiar looking, made out of brass with one lens slightly longer than the other. It appeared almost as if it had been a spy glass with a second lens added at a later date to make them binoculars. I looked through them, and the lenses were so smudged that I couldn't see anything. They just need a good cleaning and better light is all, I thought. Unusual though they were, I turned them over and over in my hands, taking in every detail about them. I saw a small list on the inside underbelly of them with a picture of a feather followed by a series of letters, like this:

J-B M B
R F
E P G
R S
B M B
G A K

Ol' Salt noticed me looking at the list and said, "Oh, yes. I almost forgot. As the new owner of these particular Binoculars, you need to inscribe your initials in the line just as all of the other previous owners have done. It is very important that this is done, or they may not work properly."

I was perplexed and amazed. How could initials affect how a set of binoculars work? Also, binoculars were usually the kind of thing that you kept for a long time, especially a set like these. "You mean that there have been *six* owners of these Binoculars? How old are they?" I asked.

"I don't rightly know. They haven't always been binoculars. Long ago, there used to be just the one side like a spy glass used on old sailing ships. Then, the previous owner before me added the other side about seventy-five year ago," Ol' Salt said.

"You mean these are *seventy-five years old*?!" I said.

"The new side of 'em is. The original part is well over three hundred years old," Ol' Salt said.

"Shouldn't they be in a museum, then?" I asked.

At this comment, a brief flash of anger crossed his face, but not for long. He then more lovingly smiled and said, "Nah. Then nobody would get th' use out of 'em. You must understand, child." He stooped down on one knee and looked kindly into my eyes. "These have to be *used to learn* and *loved*. Do you understand?"

"I'm not sure that I do entirely, but I will take care of them the absolute best that I can." I said.

"Your best is all you can give, child. Just be sure that you *are* giving your best. Don't make excuses, guard these with your life, and *use* them." Ol' Salt said. "Oh, and one last thing, this is *very* important. Each time you are done using the Binoculars, return to the *exact same place*." This also seemed like an unusual thing to say, but I was getting used to strange advice coming from this old man. At the same time, these strange words made him sort of endearing. I wondered why it was so important.

He then turned to Grandpa, whose eyes were as big as saucers and his face very serious, but it changed to a smile as soon as he noticed I was looking his way.

"Well, Ichabod, it seems my time may be coming to an end after all these years. I want to give something to you, as well." He handed Grandpa a key. "It's to this old place, that door there," he pointed to the back door where we had come in. "I plan on going back to England on a nice, slow ship to see what's become of my family before I die. I don't reckon I'll be comin' back here ever again. Thanks again for the help all those years ago. You were a life saver." And with that, we left. He watched us as we walked out, and seemed both sad and excited at the same time.

Once outside, we got into Grandpa's car. I checked my watch and saw that it was almost noon. We would get home just in time for lunch.

"We've got a stop to make on the way home," Grandpa said hurriedly.

"Where are we going?" asked Ned.

"To the store at the Audubon Bird Sanctuary. I want to get a small pair of binoculars for everyone in the family that doesn't have any," Grandpa said.

"Wow, cool! Two presents in one day! It's like Christmas," Ned said. Then he looked at my beat up old leather case, scrunched up his face and said, "I bet mine work!" I let him think what he liked. I knew that there was something special about my old Binoculars.

I thought that getting binoculars for all of the grandchildren was a nice gesture, but couldn't help wondering if it was also to lessen the attention others would give to my new gift. I got the feeling that Grandpa didn't want a lot of people to know about it.

"How did you know Ol' Salt, Grandpa?" I asked after a bit of silence on the car ride back. "I helped him out several years ago when he was hurt in a bad way," Grandpa said.

"How was he hurt?" I asked.

"He was stuck under something with a broken leg. There was no one else around to help, so I pulled him out, set his leg, and took care of him until he was better. I have seen him here and there over the years, and we have had an interesting friendship," Grandpa said.

"But, Grandpa, you aren't a doctor," I said.

"In this case, it didn't matter. I was just someone in the right place at the right time to help a neighbor in need. Sometimes that's what matters more than anything," Grandpa said.

"Yes, but—" I said.

"Well, here we are back at the house. I'm sure your wonderful Mother will have your lunch ready. You'll both want to go in and chow down before bird watching this afternoon. Especially you, Ben," Grandpa said, and he looked at me with a knowing glance.

"But I want to know more about—"

"Nonsense. You need to know about *food* right now. The *right* kind is waiting for you up those stairs," Grandpa said, winking as he spoke. It was then I was sure I was in for something different, but what?

V. Birding

We ate quickly, and were pretty excited to go out bird watching, all except Ned. "We have to be quiet all of the time, and it's really boring. Maybe I won't go." said Ned. I wasn't going to argue with him. I wanted to clean and try out my Binoculars without anyone around.

My Uncle Bob is an amateur photographer, and he had a nice cleaning set for his cameras, as well as a carbon-tipped tool for engraving. I asked to borrow it, and went into the bathroom upstairs so as not to be bothered. I read some instructions on how to clean camera lenses, took the special brush pen and cleaned off the dust from the lenses of the binoculars. After that, I sprayed a little compressed air on them to clean them off more completely. The glass was a lot clearer than it had been. It looked as if they hadn't been cleaned in years. I lifted the lenses to my eyes, but still couldn't see very well through them. I was inside, so I figured that they would be better once I was outside in the sunlight.

Next, I began to engrave my initials in the long list of the owners on the Binoculars. I wondered who all of those people were, and how long each of them had actually owned these Binoculars.

Were they really 300 years old? I felt like I was holding a precious piece of history, and had it not been for Ol' Salt's objections, I probably would have given them to my Dad to put in a museum. But the old man was insistent on them being used, so off we were going to bird-watch. Just as I finished the capital "A" for my last name, I felt something strange, like a sudden jolt of electricity, and for a second was sure that I could see my own initials glowing on the Binoculars. Then, it was gone. I sat there wondering if what I had just seen had been real, when I heard a voice calling to me.

"Ben! It's time to go!" Dad called up the stairs. I called back down, "All right. I'm coming." I carefully wrapped up the Binoculars in the cloth, made a mental note to wash that old rag sometime, and then positioned them carefully in the leather case labeled GAK.

We got to the Audubon Bird Sanctuary section of the island in the early afternoon, right in the warmer part of the day. It was a perfect day for bird watching. We all got out, and my plan was to either move ahead of the group or lag behind so I could actually see some birds. There were some pretty amazing creatures here on this part of the island. The Beach Board had put up a boardwalk on some of the trails, but I wanted to get to the footpaths as soon as possible, and get deep into the forested parts. That was where the really cool, unusual birds were.

Dad got everyone together and arranged for us all to meet back at this spot at 5:00PM. It was 1:15 in the afternoon. He recommended staying with a buddy, just in case. Dad was always safety conscious in the woods. I thought it was overkill here, and planned to ditch everybody as soon as possible.

Just then, a familiar loud, obnoxious voice broke the revered silence that is reserved for forested places like this. "This is awesome!" exclaimed Ned. There was a fluttering of wings in the trees all around us as birds retreated into the woods.

"I thought you weren't coming," I said. "I thought all of this was too *boring* for you."

"That was before my Dad gave me this really cool flip camera." Ned said. "It's got a ton of Megapixels, and can take video, I can even take it underwater. It's got a zoom, too. It's way better than those dusty old Binoculars you've got."

"I'm glad you're so happy about it." I said flatly, looking down at my old worn out case. "The best birding trail is that one over there." I said, and pointed to the one that led around a swamp. There was a small part of me that was hoping he would go for it, and that an alligator would get him.

"Great! Let's go!" Ned said, and darted loudly down the path with his camera pointing at everything in the woods.

I immediately headed for the furthest trailhead from that path that I could until I heard behind me, "Hey, wait up! I thought you said that the other way was the best way." It was Ned.

"I did. There are always lots of cool birds over that way. Besides, you might see an alligator." I said.

"Cool. So let's go that way. I'm going to stick with you, my favorite cousin! I told your Dad we would be buddies!" said Ned. I wished that he would make up his mind if he liked me or not, but I figured he just didn't want to be alone.

My heart sank. Every time that I thought I could have a brief moment to myself, Ned barged in uninvited. Oh, well. I guess I just had to make the best of it. Dad's advice was really starting to get on my nerves, but deep down, I knew he was right. Besides, I knew if I resisted Ned, he'd be even more annoying and scare away the birds for everybody in the area.

So I said, "Okay. We'll be a team. But I usually see lots of cool birds on these trips, and it's because I do it alone and am as quiet as a mouse. We will break off from the rest of the group as soon as possible. You have to be quiet on this trip, or I will disappear and leave you in the dust. I know these woods very well. In the meantime, watch out for snakes and alligators."

"Snakes and alligators?" Ned said.

"Yes," I said coolly, hoping he would be getting scared.

"Cool. I'll keep my camera out. I'd love to get a gator on video. I'll put it on Youtube!" Ned shouted.

"Great, now come on, and from now on, NO TALKING!" I said in a heated whisper.

"Okay," he whispered, and made a motion of zipping his lip. I nodded my head and we both headed down the path.

We walked on for about a half mile. It was the quietest I had ever heard him be in my life. He kept looking through the viewfinder of his flip camera. I looked at his nice, new camera, and then looked down again at my old worn out case, and was envious. I wondered if I could see anything at all out of these old Binoculars. We reached the swamp and there was a little wooden deck overlook built a few steps up for wildlife watching. I went up there and sat down on a bench built on it, motioning to Ned to do the same.

"Now what?" Ned asked, in an almost imperceptible whisper.

"We wait," I said.

"For what?"

"Birds."

"I knew this was going to be *boring*," Ned said, exasperation in his whispered tone.

I just put my finger over my lips and savored the moment, feeling great satisfaction in actually succeeding in shutting Ned up. It was worthwhile, too, because it wasn't long before some bright white large birds flew by and landed in the swampy water in front of us. They were chattering on about something, and I wondered what. Carefully, I pulled out my Binoculars, and Ned began filming one particular kind of bird. We learned that they were White Ibises when we watched the video later. They were beautiful, all walking slowly through the brackish water pecking at little creatures for food. Pretty soon, other birds came, and the swamp area was filled with Great herons, Snowy Egrets, and White Ibises.

This time, as I brought the Binoculars up to my eyes, I saw another marking, right inside the eyepiece. It read:

30:1

I hadn't noticed it before, and once again turned over the Binoculars in my hands, enjoying them, marveling at my own initials being the last in a long line of them. Again I wondered who all of these initials belonged to. When I glanced up, Ned was looking at me like I had two heads or something, and he just shook his head and went on filming the Ibises. There were scores of them, all searching through the waters for small crayfish to eat. It was a beautiful sight.

Just then, I heard something familiar that I hadn't expected. It was a hum that I had last heard on my back porch in Arkansas in August, and was surprised to hear it in this area with all of these shorebirds around. I looked around wildly to identify that the sound indeed belonged to that which I was thinking.

Ned could see I was agitated about something, and asked me silently, "What?" by shrugging his shoulders and holding one palm face-up while the other hand continued filming. I shrugged in answer, as if to say, "I don't know." But I did know. Nothing in the world makes a sound like that except for...and then I saw him: a Ruby-Throated Hummingbird.

I got Ned's attention and pointed to the hummingbird, but he was more interested in filming the Ibises, so he motioned for me to go and check out the hummingbird on my own. He was panning left and right as I slowly walked down the steps back onto the path, following the hummingbird to some bright orange flowers shaped kind of like little trumpets. The hummingbird noticed me, and didn't seem to worry too much. He was too interested in the nectar of the flowers.

The hummingbird fascinated me. I had always wanted to know where these little guys go in the winter time. I had no idea that they came here. It was amazing to see one up close right here. I drew my Binoculars up to my eyes, lined up the line with the bird as Ol' Salt had shown me, and almost without thinking, broke one of my own rules for birding and spoke softly aloud, "I wonder where you go, little one. I'd love to go with you and find out."

Immediately, everything began to change. There was a light on the ground, and when I looked at the Binoculars, I saw that the light was emanating from them. I turned them over, and was almost blinded by…my initials? There they were, shining out from the Binoculars. At the same time, they were flattening out, changing color to a pale rust color, and were *actually pushing into my throat and collarbone*. I was worried that they would choke me and tried to push them away, but strangely enough, it didn't hurt at all.

My clothes became like a scuba divers' wet suit, very tight, and soon were like skin. My own skin was rippling all over, and the hair on my arms began to thicken and grow violently fast, becoming shafts of feathers, changing color as they grew. My legs were growing shorter and shorter, and changing shape to form claws. My nose became shorter as well until all I had left was a small hole on either side of my mouth. Wait! My mouth, my mouth! My lips became hardened, and kept stretching forward in an uncontrollable kissing motion, and kept getting longer and longer, until I felt like I was looking down the barrel of a rifle. My head was getting smaller, too, and with its size adjustment my vision was altered, so that I could see more to the side than straight ahead. My peripheral vision was replaced with hind-sight and above-sight, and soon I could see almost every direction around me, even up without moving my head.

My arms involuntarily moved back behind me and up, as if I were preparing to dive into a pool for a swim meet, and my hands literally became wings as the thick hairs that had become shafts of feathers grew until they were proportionate with the rest of me, with my arm bones stopping about halfway up the wing. My breathing was faster, and I felt like my heart was beating faster than ever. I felt warm all over, and pretty soon, I was standing on the ground as…a small hummingbird just a few inches tall, weighing less than the weight of a penny.

VI. A World I Never Knew Existed

I looked around my now immense surroundings, and realized that I had not moved one inch from the spot where I had uttered those last words with the Binoculars. Oh, NO! Would those be the last words I ever said? What was to become of me? A thousand questions rushed into my head, but there was something else that was taking over. All of a sudden, I wanted to travel again, I could feel that the Sun was going to go down soon, and it was going to be cold. I needed food, the *right* food, now, and had an overwhelming desire to drink from the flowers nearby.

I tried to move. Nothing. I couldn't budge at all. I looked down at my pitiful legs and now proportionately large toes. The hunger was getting stronger. I needed to eat something soon, or my body wouldn't have enough energy for the trip. What trip? And then, it hit me. I was beginning to feel the yearnings of the hummingbird. If this had been happening to someone else, I would have thought it the coolest thing in the world. But right now, I felt nothing but helplessness. What if a snake comes out right now and wants a little snack? I've got to get off of this ground. But how? I can't walk, and I didn't think to ask Ol' Salt how to fly. For some reason, it just didn't cross my mind, then.

Ol' Salt! I needed to think about *exactly* what he had said. All of that strange advice he had given was beginning to make a little sense, now. I wished that I had listened better and could remember more of it.

"Don't make excuses! Make sure you *are giving your best!*" Ol' Salt had said.

That was it! I had to not make an excuse for anything. Instead, I had to figure out just what was necessary to do right now. Like it or not, *I was a hummingbird*.

The trees were immense, and I needed to get into them. I had to fly. This was going to be tough. Baby birds had lots of time to learn, grow, and be fed by their Mother, but I had to figure it out before something came after me. Pretty soon, something did.

I heard what seemed like inordinately loud steps shaking the ground, and was sure that there was an elephant coming down the path. It was calling out, like a sound I had heard before, but strange now. It sounded like a recording in slow motion, and was shouting very loudly, "BBBBBAAAAAYYYYYYUUUUNNNNN". Soon, I could clearly see a large, two-legged creature holding some kind of box with a circle on it in his hand. My first thought was, "I can't eat that. I wish he would have brought something useful, like a flower or some nectar."

Of course, it was Ned. He had realized I had been gone for a while, and had come looking for me. Wait a minute. What would Ned do? In that moment I was scared that he might just stomp me into the ground, so I decided to try to speak to him first. I shouted up to him when he got close enough, "I'm down here, you silly boy!"

But to no avail. All Ned heard was a chattering sound from a hummingbird. Our communication was broken, although I could sort of understand his speech. I noticed that his voice was really strange, that he still was whispering, and had been all along. It just seemed really loud to my new ears. I tried to hop, but my legs weren't strong enough. All I did was fall over. Thankfully, it was enough to get his attention.

Instead of reaching out to help me, a red light came on the box he was holding, and the circle part was pointed straight at me. He spoke. "WWWEEEYUUUULLLL, WWWHHHAAATT HHHAAAVVV WWWEEE HHHEEERRRRE?" Of course he would rather take video of me than help me.

After much effort, I was able to stand again, using my wings to get up. I told him to put the camera down and help me onto a branch, but he just kept filming. I spread my wings and started to flap, but that just knocked me over again. I righted myself once again, and this time spread my wings together and moved them up and down to get his attention.

A remarkable thing happened. Although I felt like I was just moving my hands up and down naturally, my wings automatically moved in a sort of figure eight pattern, at a speed so fast that I could hardly see or feel them moving. I was able to hover about an inch off of the ground, and soon by changing the angle of the pattern I was able to move slowly forward, or slowly backward. It felt magical, floating like that. Ned must have liked it too because he made a comment that he wished I could see this. He would never have believed that he was filming his cousin's process of learning to fly as a bird. I tried to get higher and higher, but I just couldn't get more than an inch above the ground.

Ned noticed that I could hardly move, and decided to come closer. I tried to get away, and fell over again, and he did something I never expected. He set his beloved camera on the ground, and cautiously slid his hand under me so that I was perched on his index finger, all the while making soothing sounds to try to calm this little bird down. Who was this guy? This was not the Ned I had seen all of my life. This was a gentle person looking to help, his façade gone. He lifted me up with a scared and confused look on his face, not knowing what to do with me, and I motioned with my head toward the flowers. I was famished. Thankfully, he got the hint and took me over to the flowers.

He held me in front of them and I took a long drink from many of them, directing him with my bill to each one. I was instantly filled with energy, and felt I could really fly now. I needed to get to a safe place, and get there while I had the energy to do it. I bobbed my head to thank Ned, as he may have just saved my life. What a strange thought *that* was. I began to fly again, and for a brief moment, hovered right in front of Ned's face, my bill almost touching his nose, and he just stared at me with his mouth open. I was tempted to poke my bill in his mouth and grab his tongue, but I was afraid he might bite me. I slowly ascended to the branch above, leaving him there with his mouth wide open. Ned filmed for a little while longer before going on his way looking for me.

"That was the strangest thing I have ever seen," said a voice as clear as could be. "I let you have that nectar because of the big two-legged guy, but don't think it will happen again. I've got a big trip to take, and need that nectar."

"Who said that?" I asked as loudly as I could. I looked around, and couldn't see anyone now that Ned had gone. "Who said that?" I asked again.

The answer came in the form of a dive from another hummingbird straight at me. Instinctively, I used my wings to fly to the right just slightly so that he missed me.

"Hey!" I shouted. "You almost knocked me off the branch."

"That's the idea. Get out of my territory, NOW!" shouted another hummingbird with a bright red splotch on his throat. "You're another hummingbird, a Ruby-Throated one, the one I saw in my Binoculars," I said.

The thought occurred to me that I could learn from him what it means to be a hummingbird, but the idea quickly left me as he returned for another dive-bomb attack. I flew to another branch, and he kept coming. Thankfully, I could see in most directions, and could hear his hum very clearly, so it was impossible for him to sneak up on me. Then, I saw it: a limb that passed in front of a tree trunk with gnarled branches all around it in such a way that he couldn't dive bomb me anymore. I made for it, and after a bit of navigation, landed there. He came and hovered in front of me, his long bill stretched out like a sword straight at my chest, and I took my bill and made a quick upper-cut which caused him to throw his head back. He flew back at me with his bill stretched out toward me when he stopped his attack suddenly and said, "You're not worth me hurting my bill. I've got to eat the nectar and get on my way."

"Tell me this, then," I said, "How is it your territory if you are on a trip and leaving?"

"Everywhere I go is my territory," he said, and flew off.

VII. Some Answers to My Questions

I perched on the branch for a while, surveying my environment from up there, and realized that I was aware of things that didn't matter much to me as a boy. I was keenly aware of exactly how much daylight I had left: four and a half hours. I could tell where the flowers were that were good to eat within about a mile of my perch, and I could hear insects within about 100 feet of me. And the colors, oh the colors! I never knew such colors existed. There was a whole spectrum of colors that I could see that just don't exist for people. This place was simply green to me a moment ago when I was a boy, yet now everywhere I saw brighter, more vibrant colors, sometimes hiding underneath other vegetation. I stood there, fascinated, and decided that I would have to get some practice flying if I was going to be any kind of a bird.

I began with a hover. Flapping my wings in the figure eight pattern, I hovered safely above my branch. Slowly, I put a little more energy into my left arm, I mean wing, and turned to the right. I reversed it, and then turned around to the left. I increased both, and rose in the air. I decreased slightly, and descended. A change in angle, and I was going backwards. Now, for a practice run. Cautiously, I went forward to the next tree and perched there. I saw some hibiscus below me, and went down to enjoy some nectar, darting from flower to flower. This time, I could pay attention to how I was eating in a way that I couldn't before.

My bill stayed together, and I worked my tongue back and forth rapidly, drawing the nectar out of each flower. It kind of felt like I was lapping up the nectar like a dog, rather than sucking it out like a straw as I had always imagined hummingbirds drank. These flowers were very satisfying, but something was missing from my diet. What was it? I felt like I had had a meal as a person of just milk. It was filling, but I needed something else to sustain me. What else did hummers eat?

I once again felt the strong urge to get on my way on a trip to the South, but had a feeling I must prepare my body first. So, I decided to try some brief distance flight. I felt energetic enough, and flew to the top of a higher pine tree to see where I might go. I could hardly believe how far I could see, and with incredible clarity. I could just make out the little cove where our house was, several miles away. Then it hit me. Grandpa was home, and the rest of the family was here looking at birds. Maybe he could help me. I loved being a bird, but really wanted to get back to the person I really was, just a boy named Ben. So, off I went, staying just above the tops of the trees. There was no wind at all, perfect for flying. I saw a small puddle of water that was calm, and flew down close to it to take a look at myself.

When I looked into the pool, I was amazed to see a brightly green colored ruby-throated hummingbird staring back at me. Although I knew that I was a bird, actually seeing myself like this made it really sink in. I turned to the side, and could still see myself because of the location of my eyes, and a funny thing happened. My brilliant ruby throat turned rust colored, and then brown. Then, when I turned forward again, there it was, a bright red splotch across my throat. But wait, I looked closer, and realized that it wasn't in the same shape as other birds, my ruby throat was in the same exact shape as my pair of Binoculars.

I flew on and came upon a swarm of gnats. At first I was worried about getting them in my eyes, but then something made me fly straight into them, open my mouth as wide as it would go, and fly straight through them, eyes closed. A few came into my mouth, and went right down. Perfect! That was just what I needed. I turned around, and made another pass through the swarm. I kept doing this until I was satisfied. So that's what else hummers eat!

I was flying on when I saw Ol' Salt's house. Ol' Salt! Maybe he could help me. I went in through the attic where the boards were missing, flew all around the house, but no one was there. Ol' Salt was gone. I hoped I would see him again, and soon. There was a lot I needed to know.

I continued on, and was at our house in no time. I came to each window, frantically looking for Grandpa. I finally found him on the back porch, and when he saw me perched there, he came over and gave me a good, hard, look. I told him that I needed help and that I wanted to be a boy again, but just as Ned had, all he heard was a chattering bird. So, I hovered as close to the screen as I could, placing my binocular shaped red throat right at his eye level. Pretty soon, he went into the house. Great, I thought. Maybe he didn't know what was going on, and couldn't help me. I flew around the house for several minutes before I saw him again. I heard him say something to Grandma, and then he came out onto the front porch and sat down in a rocking chair. I hovered right in front of his face, bill to nose, chattering loudly. He could tell that I was asking for something, and he spoke to me, more plainly than Ned had. The speech was slow, but understandable.

"Do you need some help, my little friend?"

I nodded my head up and down, and realized that my whole body was also going up and down, hovering. On one of the upstrokes, he got a good look at the binocular shaped splotch on my throat, and his eyes widened. Then, he did something unexpected. He pulled out his cell phone. Here I was needing help in the worst way, and he was going to make a phone call! But he didn't dial anything or press any buttons, he just held the phone to his ear. Then he stared straight at me and spoke.

"So, my little friend," He said. "It looks like you are using things that need to be *used* and *loved*. I must say, you have figured it out much more quickly than most people. I'm proud of you. Some previous owners never used your new gift their whole lives, and those Binoculars sat around collecting dust for years. Such a shame. Now, you have a trip to take, and although I'm sure you are scared and have all kinds of questions, you must take it. Learn all you can before you go, but don't stay here too long. Don't allow yourself to be reckless, and you will be safe. In difficult situations, help may come from unexpected places. I would give anything to be in your wings right now, and I'm glad it's you carrying on this tradition."

"Grandpa, who are you talking to?" Grandma called out from the screen door.

"I'm on the phone, dear." He called back in to her, and then continued to me. "Build up your body before you leave, learn from others that will help you, claim territory, and defend it. Otherwise, other birds will not have any respect for you. When it is time to go, do so, and once you start, don't turn back for any reason. Don't worry about the time that you spend away. I'll help you with that. It will all work out." He turned and started to go inside. Then he seemed to remember something, and faced me again. "Oh, and by the way, you'll want to go into torpor at night. It gets a little chilly, and it will help you save up your energy for the trip. Good luck."

I wondered where torpor was. Pretty soon, Grandma brought out a hummingbird feeder filled to the top with sugar water. Grandpa said a hasty "Goodbye" into his phone, and slipped it back into its pocket. My eyes lit up when I saw the feeder. She gave it to Grandpa, who hung it up on the porch. I immediately buzzed to it and began drinking.

"Ah, he's beautiful." said Grandma. "That he is." Grandpa said, putting his arm around Grandma. They both watched as I moved from one perch to another, all around the feeder, all the while feeling energy building in my body.

"Is that sweet enough for you, little guy?" Grandpa asked. "I buzzed over to him, and bobbed my body and head up and down. "That's amazing!" Grandma said. "It's like he understands you!"

"Yes," Grandpa said. "Somehow, I think he does."

"I just love being on the island when the birds are migrating. But won't putting a feeder out tempt him to stay and not go further south?" Grandma asked Grandpa.

"No. On the contrary, it gives them much needed food along their route. Think of it like little gas stations for hummingbirds," Grandpa said.

"Well, I may get some more and place them all around the house," Grandma said. "I love hummers!"

"Yes, let's do that. I'll come too," Grandpa said. And with a wink toward me, they went inside.

There was a grove of trees that we used to play in not far from the house, so I went to investigate, now that I had discovered my own territory with the right food. I could see flowers hidden in the undergrowth that had some nectar, and had my fill. About the time that the mosquitoes started coming out, I had another feast. I decided to go closer to the house, and eat some bugs that could be pests to my family.

Having eaten enough, I was full and satisfied for the first time today, and flew all around the island, building up my strength. When I was aware that daylight was beginning to go away, I went back, had my fill at the feeder once again, and then returned to the grove of trees near my family's house. I wanted to be there when they got home. I found a spot that was quite protected, and realized how fast the temperature was dropping, even before the sun went down completely. I was getting colder and colder, and thought, should I fly south now, before it gets cold? But no, everything pointed to preparation right now. I would have to get ready. But how do I deal with the cold? I can't possibly sleep in this cold, I might not wake up. If I die as a bird, do I die as a boy? The only one who could answer this for me was gone. Then, I felt strange. Maybe I was becoming a boy again? If so, I could still climb down from this tree. My eyes involuntarily closed, I wasn't as cold anymore, and I could feel my heart slowing down. Everything was peaceful, a peace that I had never known before in my life, and although it took time, I felt like this was the answer to the cold. Suddenly I was aware of how tired all of this had made me feel. I was drifting off to something deeper than sleep, and it felt great. My head began to droop backward, and I pointed my bill straight up.

The next thing I remember, I was awake, but my eyes were closed and my heart was barely beating. When I did open my eyes about half way after several minutes, the sun was still not up, and the whole world was upside-down. What was going on? My heart slowly began beating faster, and I vibrated my wings to warm up. Anyone who saw me would have thought I was shivering to death and hanging upside down like a bat. After about twenty minutes or so, I was awake enough to realize that I had to do something about being upside down, and began to really flap my wings for flight. I did so and let go of the branch, expecting to fall hard and have to flip around on the ground, but much to my surprise I was actually flying *upside-down*! I righted myself slowly in flight, flew just above the branch, perched on it again, and decided that I should get some more sleep since there were a couple more hours before the sun was up, and the flowers were still closed.

I awakened the second time with a normal heartbeat and a voracious appetite. So that was what torpor was, not a place, but a sort of mini-hibernation. I immediately flew to the feeder, eating mosquitoes with gusto along the way. I was grateful to have my own territory.

VIII Migration South

The next several days were spent eating constantly, and after a few days I realized that I was eating about three times my body weight each day. I exercised by taking several flights the length of the island and back. My goal was to get to the point where I could fly back and forth twenty times in a day. The island was about 14 miles long, so doing this would be great preparation for the migration flight, which I knew had to be taken, both from the yearnings within me and the advice of my Grandfather.

I was reminded on these flights of some of the information that an airplane pilot had shared with us in my class a few weeks before our trip. He had talked about how in a plane, you were part of the air. If the wind was behind you, you added speed, and when it was coming at you, your speed decreased accordingly. I was blown away by how fast I could fly east one day when the winds were strong from the west. I must have been going well over 50 miles an hour, and when you're only a few inches tall that's *really* fast. But when I got to the other end and began the return flight, I could hardly get any speed up at all, and had to stop several times and rest. One thing was for sure, I didn't want to make the trip with a headwind with the winds in front of me. I wanted a tailwind, with the winds pushing me in the right direction—south. After about two weeks of practice, I felt about ready to go. This was good, because I could tell that not only were the nights getting colder, they were getting longer, too. The longer nights made me want to leave as soon as possible and hopefully get to a place where the days and nights were a little more equal in length.

More and more birds came from all over the continent. First all male hummingbirds that constantly fought over territory, flowers, and feeders, and then as the males left one by one, the females began to show up, with fewer males still here. I practiced my dive bombing skills on leaves that were jutting out from different plants, and soon became a great territory defender. One day as I was practicing, I realized that a female had been watching me as I dove.

A female hummingbird is much more attractive when you are a bird yourself. They appear dull to the human eye, but it is just this "dullness" that makes them so beautiful to the male hummingbird. One male ruby-throat put it to me this way: "We are bright and colorful because the ladies need to see us. When I choose a mate, it's one that I want to be able to blend in and protect the children. That's what matters to me," he had said. The lady hummingbird raises the babies alone, so that made sense to me, too. They are bigger than us guys, and have longer bills, too. I thought that if they wanted to, they could beat any male hummingbird in aerial combat, but they didn't seem interested in that.

As the lady hummers arrived, I discovered that they weren't nearly as territorial, and they shared food at the feeders with many at a time. One day, one said to me, "I'm surprised you haven't already gone south. You'll need to stake out your territory at the other end." I hadn't thought about that. I hoped I could learn something from her by asking a few questions. There were some things I really wanted to know before leaving. I felt strong enough now, and believed I could make the journey, since now I had made twenty back and forth flights on a calm day without stopping.

"How do you know which way to go on the journey?" I asked.

"Oh, you'll just know. The only thing that you really need to be sure of is the wind. At this time of year, winds change from north to south. You don't want to be out there on your trip and have them change on you. It makes it a lot harder," she said.

"How can I tell if the winds will be with me the whole way?" I asked.

"You can't perfectly, but do you feel the pressure changing in your head?" she asked.

I did, but had no idea what that meant. I just nodded.

"Pretty soon, you will know how to read those pressure changes, and follow the high pressure," she said. "The weather is better when the pressure is higher. Be more careful when you feel the lower pressure."

"But how high do you fly?" I asked. "I've never made the trip before."

"Boy, you don't know anything, do you? You must be a juvenile, and arrived here early. Here I thought you were full grown, and had gotten here late. There goes one now, look at him," she said. I looked, and could barely make out a tiny hummer about 300 feet and climbing. "He'll climb as high as he can, and then choose his own altitude all the way to the big peninsula." That was the first time anyone had given me a straight answer about where I was going. My body weight was built up, and I was really practiced at flying. Now I just needed to go. But I wanted to get as many questions answered as possible.

"You mean, you go *alone*, not in flocks? How is that safe?" I asked.

"Predators have a hard time seeing us individually. If we travel in groups, they come after us. But when we go alone, we are almost invisible. The only safe flock to be in is one of small birds that won't eat us. Still, be on the lookout, especially while you are close to shore," she said. That all made sense to me, and by now I had completely lost track of the male that had just left. It was like he had disappeared.

"Anything else a first-timer needs to know?" I asked her.

"That's all I knew when I went the first time," she said.

"How many times have you made the trip there and back?" I asked.

"Four," she said.

"Then that's good enough for me; but there's something I need to do first though," I said.

Instinct as well as watching other birds taught me to preen before I flew, and it was going to be even more important before this long flight. I ruffled my feathers and fluffed myself out as much as possible. I put some oil from my preen gland on my bill and began nibbling along each feather to clean myself of dirt, oil, and those nasty parasitic mites. I particularly went over my flight feathers, making sure that they would stay together by working the oil into each feather. I scratched all over with my little claws, and cleaned my bill off of the sticky nectar on some nearby green leaves. As I ruffled again, each of my 923 feathers (I actually counted them a few days before as I perched on a limb and wondered how many feathers I had) fell perfectly into place, and I was more aerodynamic, ready for my big flight! I lowered my head, fanned my tail, and took off for Grandpa and Grandma's house.

I went to the house and chattered away, hoping to see Grandpa and Grandma. They came out, and I did a brief dive bomb exercise for them. They were delighted. Grandpa looked me over, saw how I had changed since he had first seen me, and said, "You're ready to make the journey." More than anything, that was what I needed to hear. I took one last long drink at the feeder, and began climbing into the sky, eating a few last minute bugs in my ascent. I remember that the winds had shifted just the night before, and now were blowing from the north to the south, perfect for my start. I looked at the sun and could tell that I had 11 hours worth of daylight left. I hoped that was enough to make the flight I needed to take. I had been keeping track of the days, and the best I could tell, it was the middle of October.

I began a slow ascent as I flew south, and climbed higher and higher. Nothing in the world is quite as euphoric as the feeling you get when you climb, really climb into the air. Now I understood what the pilot who had come to my class meant when he told us how every takeoff made him feel. I climbed slowly, wanting to get as far as possible in the climb out, to save energy.

It wasn't long before I was flying over the huge expanse of ocean, and the seashore was long gone. I saw some pelicans gliding near the surface of the water, a magnificent example of a flyer from a bygone age, floating like a pteranodon below me looking for fish. Occasionally, a loggerhead turtle would come up to the surface of the ocean for breath. As I was gazing down at one, I came to a part of the air that was hotter than the rest, and I began to rise faster without any more work. I remembered watching hawks and eagles climb these thermals back in Arkansas, making lazy circles and climbing without so much as a single flap of their wings. Not me. Just to stay up, I was beating my wings at least 50 times a second, and to make good time, I would beat them much faster.

Soon I could tell that I had climbed as high as I was going to go, because my wings were just keeping me at the same flight level, and I couldn't risk wasting my energy climbing when I had so far to travel. "The peninsula," she had said. Surely that was the Yucatan Peninsula, that part of Mexico that sticks out into the west side of the Gulf. I remembered seeing it on the globe one day while looking at the Gulf of Mexico with my Dad before we came to the island. Still, that was a long way to go, although I didn't know exactly how many miles.

It was gorgeous up here, blue sky meeting blue sea in a perfect horizon as far as the eye could see. I seemed to be hardly moving at all, although the wind was stronger up here, and was pushing me very quickly away from shore. I could clearly see pods of bottle-nosed dolphins traveling here and there, and was just coming to the first line of natural gas rigs that are visible from shore. I flew over them, and saw a small flame coming out of the top of each one, and heard a very loud tone sound every few seconds while I was near them. There were a few bugs by them, and I ate as many as I could, not sure if I would get any more food for a while.

As I kept flying, it became harder and harder to stay at the same altitude. Not sure how high my flight should be I decided to descend fairly close to the water in order to see the marine life better. I began a long, slow descent, which helped my speed and distance, because gravity was with me. I thought that I would draw this out as long as possible. I had flown so far now that I couldn't see the shoreline anymore. I wasn't sure how long I had flown, but the words of that visiting pilot came back to me: "Long flights are hours of beautiful scenery and uninterrupted peace separated by moments of sheer terror." I was enjoying the former, and hoped to do without the latter.

My descent took a really long time, and I was sure I had traveled at least a hundred miles by the time I had come down almost to the surface of the water. I was starting to have a pretty good idea how Charles Lindbergh must have felt all by himself in his airplane flying over the Atlantic all those years ago. I had done a report on him last year in the fourth grade, and remembered a lot of the things he had done on his flight. It was a lot different making a long flight with no plane, but on your own actual wings.

I wanted to see any kind of life that I could, and so chose to travel about 20 feet or so above the water. The winds were still from the north to the south, the horizon was as beautiful as ever, and the water was getting clearer and clearer. Then, I saw them. At first I thought I was seeing things. Something small was far off, flying just above the water, and then was gone. Then another, and another jumped out of the water, flew along for a while, and returned into the sea. What were these little things? They weren't birds, I was sure of that. I kept flying lower and lower to get a better look and eventually a flying fish flew along beside me for about two hundred feet, and I watched him as he used the updrafts from small waves to get lift and fly farther. I began to do the same thing, and it made flying that much easier. I kept seeing them for miles on end, and enjoyed the company on this long flight.

After seeing the flying fish, I was getting excited about what else I might see, but nothing could have prepared me for what was about to happen. I flew on for a couple of hours seeing nothing but blue sea with an occasional shadow swimming down deep, and began to hear a strange, high pitched sound that I had never heard before in my life. This sound was soon accompanied by a series of clicks that were emanating from the water all around me. What was this sound? Then they surfaced. I saw fins come up out of the water, and instinctively climbed to stay out of the way, just in case it was a group of sharks. I had seen a school of hammerheads on a fishing trip with Grandpa and Dad once. But these were moving like they were breathing air, with regular intervals coming up and down like bottle nosed dolphins, and there were lots of black dorsal fins, not grey, some of them so tall that they were falling over.

I climbed a little, all the while looking down at the incredible scene that was unveiling itself before me. Just then, two killer whales came halfway out of the water together, breathing in perfect harmony, mouths looking as if they were smiling. I climbed still higher, and saw that it was a large pod, or family of them. They must be lost, I thought. I had read about the Orcas' travels once in a nature magazine, and the article I read talked about them ranging from Alaska down through the cold Pacific Ocean, but in the warm waters of the Gulf of Mexico?! Yet here they were. I couldn't deny it. I began to count them for something to do, and reached 30 in this one group. Then as I looked, about a mile away I saw another pod, not quite as large, but still it had a lot of whales, at least 20 more over there.

The whales were very playful with each other, and seemed to be having a great time. I decided to descend further and get a closer look. The sound I had heard before returned and got louder as I came nearer to the surface of the water, and I noticed that each of them had different markings on their fins and sides. Curiosity got the better of me and I got close enough to see their real eyes that sat right in front of their uniquely shaped large white eye patches. I was debating about getting even closer to them when suddenly two whales came completely out of the water right in front of me. Could their sonar pick up small objects flying above the water?

The one closest to me vaulted its entire body up out of the water, breeching fully. Time seemed to stop as for the briefest of moments I was nose to nose with a killer whale about 20 feet long and several thousand pounds! My already fast heartbeat was going a mile a minute, thudding in my ears in terror as I wondered if this magnificent animal would eat a small bird for a tiny morsel of a snack. I could feel the air disturbed around me even as he surfaced, and instinctively flew up as high as I could and a little to the side just as his massive body came toward me. I got a good look at him as he passed through the air. His white eye patch was a little wider at the back, kind of like a big pear. His real eye looked straight at me as he continued his flying arc out of the water, and it seemed to be filled with intelligence and understanding that I had never seen in any other creature on earth. The whole thing probably really only lasted a couple of seconds, but it was an eternity to me. My heart then seemed to stop for a split second as I looked straight at the head of this majestic creature expecting it to gobble me up, but its mouth never opened, and I realized that I had dodged it successfully.

As he descended back towards the water, I saw that his back had a grayish mark in the shape of a flying bird that wrapped around his dorsal fin. The two splashed back down in glorious fashion, almost as if they were laughing at the scare they had just given this little bird flying along and only just missing me with their spray of seawater. I continued to fly higher, and they began a frenzy of jumping out of the water all over the place. They seemed to be playing together, and the entire ocean was their playground. As I flew away from them, they were on their sides, splashing their pectoral fins. Wow! No one was ever going to believe this, but then again I wasn't sure how much of this trip I would ever be able to share with anyone.

I had to part company with them and continue on my own journey as they were going east, following a school of tuna that I hadn't noticed until I had climbed up to get a better look at the playful Orca. I continued on South, hoping for landfall, because as exhilarating as all of this was, I was beginning to get a little tired. A little nectar would be nice, too, but I had to put that out of my mind until I got somewhere that had some, and that may be a while yet.

As I continued to fly along, the pressure in my head changed, and I became uneasy about continuing my flight. This was bad, as I was out over the ocean with nowhere to land. I noticed that there were more and more clouds developing in front of me, and they were quickly changing from the puffy, pretty clouds that you can imagine pictures in to the larger, greyer rain clouds. There was a pretty dark spot indicating hard rain traveling from West to East directly across my path, and it wasn't long before I began to feel it. The rain began falling in great big drops at first, and I was headed right into the heaviest part of it. I climbed while I still could, so that the downward force of the rain as well as the additional weight from getting wet would not drive me straight into the water and drown me. I was thankful that I had preened right before I left, and the thin layer of oil was doing its job of rolling the water off of me—for now. The winds changed constantly, and soon I couldn't tell what direction they were coming from at all. It was then that I realized how deep the instinct was inside me to stay on course. I still can't explain it, but I was able to get through the driving rain with my eyes only half open. It was getting harder to keep the wings going at the former speed because they were heavier from being wet, which meant my oil was coming off. On the other hand, it was nice to have a bath in fresh water, and it cooled me down on this warm day out in the gulf. I also discovered that if I opened my mouth, I could drink some of it. It wasn't nectar, but it was something. I hadn't eaten anything since the last few bugs I had seen swarming back near the natural gas rigs.

Through the driving rain, I could see a shape on the water in front of me. I couldn't quite make out what it was, but it seemed to be a ship of some kind. I wasn't sure how far I would be able to go in this rain, and it was traveling from East to West, so I veered a bit off course to the east, and made for it. I had to fly higher to land on it, and I was able to get in under some deck stairs and stay dry. I hoped that the combination of the movement of the ship and the movement of the storm would mean that the rain wouldn't last long, and I could continue my flight south.

It seemed like hours waiting under that step, but it probably was only about 20 minutes or so. I just wanted to hold my course safely. Also, I knew now that I only had about three hours of light left, and I planned to make the best of it. I was thankful for the chance to rest my wings, and spotted something I hadn't planned on when I had seen the ship. There were little black ants on the deck in front of me, going to and from somewhere on board, no doubt the dining area. I didn't think anyone would mind, so I had a little protein snack while I waited for the storm to pass by.

From the ship, I could see flashes of lightning out on the water, and was struck by how profoundly beautiful it was. An awesome display was right before my eyes, but I hadn't been able to enjoy it until I was out of the storm myself. And then it stopped, just as quickly as it had begun and soon became nothing more than a dark spot on the horizon moving away from the ship. So now I had to get in the air. I still had miles to go, and not much daylight left.

I shivered my wings as soon as the rain stopped, trying to get off as much water as possible. I preened quickly once more and took off, flying over the ship, thanking God for the chance to have a place to land, and moved on. The ship was filled with cargo containers and was huge. I wondered where it was headed. I noticed that I was not alone, there were other birds that had hitched a ride, but they stayed closer to the ship once I made my escape.

Pretty soon I was all alone again. I ascended as I had done at the beginning of my flight, but not nearly as high. I just wanted to get a look around and then use gravity to make some speed and distance. I got to the point I had been before, having bought about 30 miles from my slow descent, and continued on my southward course. The water was much calmer than I had expected it to be after the storm, and clear right down to the bottom.

It was then that I saw the stingrays. I had learned the difference between stingrays and manta rays because they were so common in the Gulf of Mexico. The difference was that the Manta couldn't sting you. The Manta has a very small tail almost like a thick hair, and has two short, stubby parts that jut out in the front to form its mouth. Sometimes they jump out of the water when they are feeding or playing. The stingray, of course, has a thicker tail. What I didn't know was that stingrays swam in schools. This school was huge. They were all going the same way, due south, and there were thousands of them. It was beautiful. They really are elegant creatures as they glide along on their golden wings. I was low enough to see that they were different from the ones I had always seen on the island, their noses looked kind of like the nose of a cow. I enjoyed the sight for quite a while until I had flown past them, and for a long time, the peaceful image of them stayed with me. This was by far the most amazing nine hours I had ever spent in my life, and the trip was only about half over.

The sun was descending rapidly to the west and a little south, and had filled the sky with more colors than I knew existed. To humans, some of them don't exist, and the incredible beauty of this sight was beyond words. Once the sphere of the sun was down, I knew that it would be harder to navigate until the stars came out. Once it was fairly dark, for there was no moon up yet, I noted that on the horizon there seemed to be an island. My eyes must be playing tricks on me. I know that in the desert, people often see mirages of oasis. Is it possible that in the middle of this fading light of day that I was seeing a mirage of an island? It was just at the very edge of my vision of the horizon, but it was definitely there. I kept flying, and soon it could not be mistaken. There was in front of me a long string of grass stretching for about a mile and just a few feet across. I headed for it. It was dark, and I needed to rest again.

IX. On to Mexico and Discovery

I reached the little island, and was greeted by hundreds of birds bedding down for the night. They were mainly gulls and gannets. I was glad to be a small hummingbird, so finding a spot wasn't that hard. The little floating island was nothing more than a high mat of floating grass that due to tides and winds and waves had connected together over time. The grass in the mat was only about four to five inches at its highest point, but there were logs and debris that had a small amount of grass growing a bit taller. Although I couldn't see them in the dark, I could tell that there were some big creatures in the water under this floating stuff.

I was appreciative of this little spot, but didn't want to spend more time than I had to here. It was a place to rest, that was all. I had a feeling that there was danger here, too. So I buried myself into a part of the grass that was denser and higher than other parts, leaving myself two ways out just in case another bird decided I would taste good. Most of the other birds here seemed just as tired as I was, but that also probably meant that they were as hungry as I was, too, and that may not be a good thing for me, one of the smaller birds. I decided not to torpor, I needed to be alert here. Besides, the temperature was perfect.

I awoke at the first hint of light before the sphere of the sun had come over the horizon, and felt very refreshed. The half moon had risen while I slept, and gave off a dull light. I felt something moving at my feet, and immediately fluttered back a few inches. As I looked down, there were tiny bugs of a very strange shape crawling around on the stalks of grass along with tiny crabs. I wasn't sure if I could eat the crabs, but I had a few of the bugs, and the food along with the sleep really strengthened me. I was now ready to fly on. I headed out, hoping that my hum didn't attract any would-be predators. I was still hungry, and noticed this morning that I was lighter than I had been yesterday, all of that flying was making me lose weight. I had to get on my way so that I could fuel up at the other end.

There was hardly any wind today, so my time would be slower than yesterday. I was curious to know more about this place, so I hovered low for a moment and looked into the clear water. There seemed to be little grape-like structures all in the bottom line of the sea grass, and I wondered if that was what made it float. I saw hundreds of smaller fish schooling near the surface, and just as I was trying to decide what kind they were, a large gulf dolphin, or mahi-mahi, came quickly out from under the sea grass to the surface and had a quick meal of many of them. I backed up, and saw many more shadows in the shape of gulf dolphins swimming along under there as well as some longer, thinner fish with pointed noses a bit deeper. The water was amazingly clear so that even in this little light I could see well into it.

Watching that dolphin eat reminded me of how hungry I was, and also that I didn't want to become anybody's snack on the migration track. So, I began once again heading south, and it wasn't long before the sun bounded up out of the sea, flooding all of the world with light, and giving me new energy in a way that was different than food. I again began to see flying fish, which I thought was a good sign. The water was a lighter shade of blue now than it had been yesterday, and I began to see fishing boats much more often, so I figured it was getting shallower and I was closing in on land. This was good, as now I had flown for about 16 hours, and hoped to see land soon. Then, I heard a splash right behind me. I looked and somehow missed what it was. Just to be on the safe side, I rose to about 30 feet above the water, well out of the reach of anything that I thought could jump out.

I was delighted to see Manta Rays jumping out of the water, and half diving, half flying back down into the water. They were of all different sizes, most of which being about 12 feet across. Each one was different in its approach to exit the water. Some took a very steep takeoff out of the water, going as high as possible, and came down with a big splash. Others took a more shallow takeoff, and then flapped or angled their bodies in a sort of a shallow upside down "u" with their "wings" pointing down to stay aloft as long as possible. There were hundreds of them, not nearly as many as the migrating stingrays I had seen yesterday, but lots of them. Then, I saw the biggest Manta that I had ever seen. It swam as if it were flying under the water slowly, came to the surface, breeched, and then descended again and was gone. It had to have been 25 feet across! It dwarfed the size of the other ones that were jumping around.

Wait a minute. These were not fish that were migrating, these were animals fishing and playing in the water! I hoped that would mean that the shoreline had to be close. I veered course just a bit to the west so that I was flying mainly south and a little west, and I was sure that landfall was not far behind. I stayed at about 30 feet until I had passed the mantas, and then went back down within about 10 feet of the surface. Pretty soon, I began to see shore birds.

Then, I saw it. After more than 18 hours of flying over the Gulf of Mexico, I could see land on the other side. My "arms" burned, and I was a *lot* lighter, but I had made it. I rose to get a better look and saw more bottle-nosed dolphin pods running along the surf. Then I saw trees! I began to think of what I would do first when I arrived. I needed to find a safe place to perch and get nectar from the flowers, and then take a well-deserved nap in my new home away from home. I had it all planned out.

Soon I would discover that I wasn't the only one who had arrived today and had made plans. As I was almost to shore along a beautiful beach with azure-blue water, devoid of any people and thinking about what a paradise this was, I got an uneasy feeling, like someone or something was watching me. I looked all around, then finally up, and saw a hawk headed straight for me, about a hundred feet above me. He had arrived a short time ago, and was as famished as I was and looking for a meal. He knew I was weak from the trip, and thought I would be easy prey. He was in a dive toward me, and as I knew I couldn't outrun him, I decided to try to outmaneuver him. I waited until my ears told me he was really close, which was only a second or two, and I moved suddenly to the side. This happened one more time with successful avoidance both times. I was now completely over the land, saw some flowers not far off, and wanted to get to them. But first I had to get rid of this hawk.

He went up for another dive, and I decided to go as close to the ground as possible, hoping to slam him into it in a similar maneuver. However, just as I was about to move to the side once again, I saw another bird coming at me from that same side, and I was trapped. I landed on the sand, and braced myself for the impact of one or the other. I bent my head forward, touched my bill to the binocular shaped ruby splotch on my throat, and closed my eyes.

As before, everything changed. There was no impact on me, for the hawk tried to pull up at the last moment when he saw I was now too large for him to eat, but too late. He careened into the sand, and was helplessly flopping on the beach, stunned. The other bird flew off before any kind of collision with either of us. Because you see, now lying on the beach was not a bird, but a boy named Ben, exhausted after having flown over 500 miles. The Binoculars were hanging around my neck. They had traveled with me the entire time I was a bird, and I was determined to keep them around my neck the entire time that I was on this journey. My senses had reverted back to those of a human, and some of the more glorious colors and sounds were now gone. Every bone in my body ached, I had lost a lot of weight, and my muscles were worn out.

X. On the Shore

I didn't know how it had happened, but at least now I knew I wouldn't be a hummingbird for the rest of my life. I thought through the last few moments, and wasn't sure what had caused the change. I hadn't *said* anything, or wished to change back. Actually, I was a little disappointed now to be a boy down here. I had been looking forward to exploring everything as a bird. I looked for other hummers, but didn't see any. At any rate, I felt too exposed out on the beach. I guess I was still thinking like a bird.

I looked at the writhing hawk on the beach, and decided to help it, although it had tried to eat me just moments ago. I couldn't blame it. I had eaten my share of helpless insects as a hummingbird. After all, it was just being a hawk, and in the end, no harm was done. So I looked it over, and discovered that it had a few damaged primary flight feathers, but otherwise it was okay. I checked to see if I still had my pocketknife with me, and was surprised to see that I did, so I snipped the feathers with the little scissors on it where they had broken. The hawk would just have to fly low and slow until these few now short feathers grew back. I noticed a scar just below its right eye, as well as a mark on its left foot, marks from a past skirmish of some sort. It had a white spot on its chest both vertically and a little horizontally so that it formed a sort of cross when its wings were outstretched. It was lucky it hadn't broken its neck. Still, if I left it here on the beach by itself unable to fly, I was sure that something would get it, and I didn't want that to happen. I helped it up, put it on my arm, took it over into the trees and set it on a branch. It stared at me for a long time. I didn't know if it was thankful or upset.

I left him there, sitting on the branch and went back toward the beach to think things over. So now what? Here I was, sitting on a beautiful beach in paradise, waves lapping gently on the shore, starving with no food or drink. I needed to find food, and fast. What was I going to eat? I looked into the crystalline water and saw fish darting to and fro in the waves. But with no hook and line, I couldn't do much. I looked around to see if I could find a sharp stick or something to catch some fish with, and looked all the way down the tide line of the beach to see if anything had washed ashore that I could use. I saw something that looked like green rope about 100 yards down the beach, and walked towards it to see what it was.

I remember my Grandpa saying rope was always good to have when you were near the sea, but I was trying to figure out how it could help me find food. As I got closer, though, I saw that it wasn't a rope at all, and ran to pick it up. It was a part of a fish net that must have gotten away from a boat and washed ashore. It was the approximate shape and size of a garbage bag. I looked it over, and saw that it was in pretty good shape, with just a couple of places that needed repair. I grabbed some small sticks and made a quick loop knot around them from the other parts of the net, and it was complete. On the way back, I spied a couple of large rocks sitting in the water, and thought it might be a good place to set up the net. Now, how could I use it to catch some fish?

I sat down on the beach to think it over, and noticed that as the waves went back out, the holes bubbled up until the wave was out. Clams! I looked around for a piece of driftwood that had a flat part that I could use as a makeshift shovel, and waited for the next wave. Spying one that would do, I grabbed it and set the net carefully down on the beach, digging after them. I remembered having a hard time doing this when I was younger, and usually missed the clam and just dug into the sand for hours. Not this time. I was so hungry that I was determined to get them! As I was digging in the area of the surf where they were, I noticed some other shells that were just sitting on the sand not far into the water. Scallops! I could almost taste them, but they would have to wait until I got these clams to a place where they couldn't just dig down again.

I took a total of about 6 clams over to a large log that had washed up on the beach with an indentation shaped kind of like the state of Idaho. I wasn't sure how to cook the clams, but I wanted to get started as soon as possible. I was so hungry that I could have eaten a raw fish right out of the ocean; scales, bones, and all, but knew that I shouldn't eat these clams raw. I took out my knife and opened the blade, inserted it firmly into the shell just inside the hinge, and sliced at the muscle that attached it to its shell. I made a mess of it, but in the end I was able to get it open and separate the meat from the guts. I placed them separately in the Idaho shaped bowl, and began cleaning the rest of them.

I needed to build a fire to cook the clams on, and as hungry as I was, gathered up driftwood like a mad person, dug a pit, whittled down some shavings like I'd learned in Scouts, and found some sea grass that was dead and placed it at the base. If I only had a magnifying glass to use the sun's rays to start it. Wait, what was I thinking? I had the Binoculars! I used their lenses to create a couple of strong beams of light from the sun, and it wasn't long before I had ignited the sea grass and wood shavings, and had a small fire going. Slowly, the dry driftwood caught, and I had a fire to cook on.

Next, I decided to try to catch some scallops while I waited for the fire to become a bed of coals to cook on. I went back for the scallops, and it seemed as if a bunch of little blue eyes were looking at me from all around the inside edge of their shells. Scallops don't dig down like clams do, so I bent down to pick up one, and it swam away from me, sort of scampering through the sea like a pair of swimming castanets.

I kept at it, and after a while was able to figure out in which direction they would swim, and was able to counter them without a problem, picking them up in my hands. Placing them in my pockets as I went, I was about to catch my seventh one when I heard a commotion near the fire. The shore birds had noticed my catch, and were beginning to hover overhead. All at once they began swooping down onto the log, and picking up the food I had worked so hard for! I ran toward them, and by the time I reached the little camp, they had taken all but three of the meat parts, and there was only one left of the other parts. So, I decided to keep everything in my pockets this time while I dug some more. I went back out and dug three more clams, so I now had six clams and six scallops.

Looking back at the beach, I saw that the fire needed tending, so I went back to the shore and added some wood in a teepee shape over the initial one. I cleaned the scallops so that all I had to eat was the marshmallow looking thing in the middle, and had the rest to use for bait! I still was hungry, and decided to try my luck fishing. I took a couple of long, thin sticks, my bait and net back out to the water. I was determined to catch something, so I put the net over by the rock, hoping that some fish were hiding under or around the rock. Weaving the sticks into the net, I stuck them deep into the sand so that the mouth of the net stayed open, cutting a notch in the top of both sticks to set the netting in to hold it. Then, I placed the bait from the clams and scallops on smaller sticks and wrapped the net line around both the bait and the sticks so that they would stay in place inside the net.

I went back to the fire, dug a trench around it, and started trying to build a spit for cooking whatever I caught in the net. In the end, I wound up whittling a couple of sticks to have sharp points because I didn't have anything that would work to lash the sticks together. I was able to cook three clams at a time on a single stick. It just seemed like they were in the fire for a moment and they were ready to eat. Clams had never been my favorite before this trip, but in this state of severe hunger, they were heavenly! I then felt like I was on a Scout campout as I took the scallops and placed them like marshmallows one at a time on each of my sticks. They cooked just as quickly, and it wasn't long before I had eaten all of the shellfish.

My hunger was helped by the clams and scallops, but now I felt like I needed something heavier that could sustain me for longer. The shore birds were beginning to take notice of my net, so I thought I would go out and see if anything was there. I moved much more slowly than I wanted to so as not to spook whatever might be there. Much to my surprise, there were eight small fish and two of something else, bigger. I couldn't quite make out what they were. They were something with a shell.

I returned in a direction that would be difficult for them to see me coming, and moved extremely slow, taking a long time to reach the net. Once there, I took hold of each of the sticks that were stuck into the sand, and in one quick jerking motion, I had the mouth of the net up. Only one fish escaped, so I was left with seven, and whatever else was in there. Was it heavy! I dragged it all up on shore to get a better look.

The net was filled with seven fish that were making a croaking noise once they were out of the water. I had caught a lot of croakers near my Grandparents' house on the island, but none ever that looked like these. I cleaned three of them with my knife, not into fillets but just so that the back part of the fish was ready to be cooked, tail and all, as we sometimes cleaned trout out of the White River back home. I then stuck the point of the stick through the meat and the skin, and put it over the fire. I was concerned that once it started cooking, the meat might separate from the skin and fall into the fire, so I was very careful. As I was cooking it, I glanced over at the crustaceans still in my net.

They were kind of like great big shrimp, only with a really hard shell, with spines all over their bodies pointing forward. They each had two huge antennae that they both kept waving around, and had stripes down their dark reddish orange bodies. There were two creamy colored spots on each of their backs, and their eyes were on stalks, like crabs. I wasn't sure if I could touch them safely because they were so spiny, and I didn't know if they were good to eat. So, I left them in the net and concentrated on cooking the fish.

Now I had a meal all prepared of fish. I don't know if it was because of my famished state or because the food was so fresh and excellent, but it was the most delicious meal I had ever tasted. It's a funny thing. Back home, I could never have eaten more than one of these little fish in one meal. But, hungry as I was from the flight, I had just eaten three fish, six clams, and six scallops! Who said eating like a bird meant you didn't eat much? It had made me eat more than I ever had as a human. The only thing missing was water. Now that my hunger was more than satisfied, I wondered what to do about my increasing thirst. As a bird, I could get some drink from the flowers, but it was much more difficult as a person.

I had more than enough food, and was just wondering what to do with the extra fish when I noticed that the hawk was still on the branch where I had left him, glaring at me. He hadn't taken his eyes off of me the entire time. I knew that he was as hungry as I was, so I grabbed two fish, and took them over to him. He ate them greedily, and continued staring at me once he was done. I told him he was welcome. Then I told him, "Don't look at me like that! Remember, it was you that first tried to eat me!" I went back to my little fire and sat down in the sand. There was a perfect spot where I could lie down in the shade and rest nearby, but I really wanted to find *some* kind of drink. I was so thirsty, I was really tempted to drink the crystal clear ocean water, but knew that if I drank very much of that salt water, I could get very sick or even die, so I resisted the temptation.

Just then I heard a voice. I looked down the beach, and saw three people coming towards me.

They were tanned, with jet black hair, all younger men in their twenties wearing Bermuda shorts and loose fitting collared shirts. One had three medium sized nets on poles in his hand; one had some long, thin, sticks; and one was pulling a cooler on wheels. They were coming right towards me! "Alo!" the one in front shouted.

I waved to them, not knowing what else to do. My hunger was satiated, but I was still worn out and had a ravaging thirst. When they got closer, the one in front said, "Hola! ¿Como Estás?" Oh, great. Of course they spoke Spanish. I was in their country, after all. Here I was, weakened after flying over 500 miles, in a country of whose language I only knew a few phrases, and had strangers coming toward me. My Dad had said, after a trip to Honduras once, that the best thing to do was try to communicate in their language in order to get them to communicate with me in mine. I decided to put a bold face on, and hope for the best. I had learned some basic Spanish in school. Now if I could just remember it. The meaning of the words came slowly to my mind, and I remembered that they were just saying, "Hello, how are you?"

"Muy bien. ¿Y tu?" I said, hoping that it was "I'm fine, and you?" They responded with something I couldn't understand, and then I remembered some other words and slowly added, "¿Hablas Inglés?" I held my breath, hoping that they would respond with something that I could understand in English.

"Jes, I a-speak-a-liddle-English," the one in front said. "We saw de –ahhh— saw de smoke from jor—" he broke off, unsure of the word, and pointed. "Fire!" I said. "Jes!" he said. "We came from Chichen Itza. It's very close. We came to see if we could find some…" he trailed off, and his eyes lit up as he saw the two crustaceans in the net.

"¡Ay, Langosta!" He shouted, and the other two men's eyes were wide with excitement as well. All of a sudden my little camp was filled with wild excited conversation in Spanish from these three men all talking at once. Finally, the excitement died down a bit and he asked, "Where ju find them?"

"Out there," I said, pointing to the rock in the water. "What are they?" I asked.

"This English word I know. *Lobster*," he said it like a maitre-d at a restaurant, eyes rolling back into his head in the sheer joy of saying the word. Something told me that he had practiced that before.

"But they don't have pinchers," I said.

"These are a-rock lobsters. Much better than pinchy America ones," he said.

"But how do you prepare them?" I asked.

"That is what we came here for. We will show you, but please, would you show me exactly where you catch them?" He asked.

I eyed their cooler, and wondered if they had any water to drink. I was so thirsty my body was beginning to hurt. I must have looked at it less subtly than I had thought, because he said, "Ju want some water? We have some."

"Sí. Please!" I said, combining both languages. They opened the cooler, got out three pairs of heavy rubber gloves and a net, and gave me a half liter bottle of water.

"¡Muchas Gracias! Thanks a lot!" I said, and proceeded to down it all at once. I felt much better after that. Now all my body needed was rest, but that would have to wait.

Overwhelmingly grateful, I motioned and said, "Come here. I'll show you where I caught those Langosta."

All three men eagerly followed me out toward the rock in the cove. Each of them now was wearing the gloves, and had a net and a long, thin stick. I began to feel a little scared walking with these unknown men out into the water, but I decided not to show it. The leader handed me a thin-meshed net with a drawstring at the top. It looked to me like a laundry bag. I was surprised that they didn't have bait of any kind.

I really wanted to learn their names. I tried to remember some words from a song I learned in the third grade about names, and after humming the music a little, asked the leader person, "¿Como te llama?" He smiled a broad, happy smile at my use of his language. This was so cool! It just seemed like a game at school when we would ask each other "What is your name?" and here I was really doing it!

He stopped, looked me straight in the eye with a big smile, placed his hand on his chest, and said, "Pedro." Then he pointed to each of the others and said, "Y Enrique, y José." They both waved. I stopped, shook their hands, and said, "¿Como estás?" with the greeting that Pedro had shown me when we first met.

They both said, "Bien, bien," and I remembered that meant fine. Although they were obviously much quieter than Pedro normally, they seemed glad to be officially introduced by name. I turned to move toward the rock, and Pedro stopped me and said, "¿Como te llama?"

"Ben," I said, eyes bright at the understanding of their language.

"Hola, Ben!" They all said with great enthusiasm.

We came closer and closer to the rock, and Pedro held up his hand for us all to stop. He acted as if he saw something that he had been looking for, and he slowly walked around it to the side of the rock where the water was much deeper. He put his stick down in the water, jiggled it a few times, set his net down, and came up with a big smile and a lobster in the net. He came over to me and placed it in the laundry bag.

I had to see how this was done. It looked like fun. I went around to the far side with José, and he pointed to a part under the rock where two long stringy things were sticking out, moving around. I recognized them as the antennae from a lobster. He placed his net in the water first, and then placed his thin stick in so that he just barely touched it from behind. It slowly moved forward. Then, he placed his net right behind the lobster, and touched it with his stick in the front. It moved backwards with amazing speed, right into the net.

I looked over at Enrique, and saw that he had caught one while I had been watching José, and Pedro had caught another one. They added their catches to the bag I was holding, and now we had four.

"Here, ju try!" Pedro said to me.

I traded the bag for his gloves, pole, and net. He pointed to a spot not far from us where some more antennae were sticking out. I did just as José had done, and sort of tickled him out from his hiding place, put my net down, and turned to touch him in front. He shot off backward with lightning speed, right under the rock. I missed him! I was disappointed. I wanted to catch one.

"It's okay," Pedro said. "We find more."

It wasn't long before we saw some more antennae, and just as before, I touched him behind, and he came out from under the rock. I kept lightly tapping him to come out farther, and placed my net right behind him. Then, I put my stick in front and was about to touch him when he shot straight backwards, right into my net. I was thrilled! I lifted my net triumphantly, and took him out with my gloved hands and examined him. He looked just as the ones I had on the beach, but when I turned him over, he had some dark orange stuff underneath his tail.

Pedro pointed to the dark orange stuff. "Eggs" he said, "It's a girl. We have to put back. The babies need to grow up." And he took it and placed it gingerly back into the water. It disappeared like a shot. By now, José and Enrique had each caught another, and Enrique noticed that his, too, was a female with eggs. He released it into the water. We stayed out there until we had a total of eight keepers, including the two that I had on the beach. I was amazed how quickly we had caught them. The bag was really heavy, now, and I was still weak from the flight. I fell once on the walk back to the fire, and Pedro took the bag from me and carried it the rest of the way.

"Ju okay?" he asked.

"I'm just tired," I said.

We brought them back to my little fire, and Pedro and the others prepared to cook them. Rather than cleaning them like other fish I had seen, he twisted them where their tail started. It came apart in his hands. He then broke off one of the big antenna at the thicker part, and proceeded to place it in a small hole by the base of the tail. Turning the antenna in the hole, he pulled firmly, and out came the vein of the tail. He then returned the head and body portion to the sea, and did the same with all of the others.

They opened the cooler again, got out some large scissors, and cut the fins off of the tail. They asked to use my pointed sticks, and stuck them through the tails on the sticks, cooking them over the coals at the base of the fire. I took out my knife, and whittled two more sticks, and the four of us sat there in silence, watching the fire, and letting the scent of fresh lobster waft into our heads.

After just a few minutes the lobster tails were cooked, and we ate them quietly, listening to the gentle waves on the shore. Nothing encourages silence among people like good food. I hadn't felt hungry after all that I had already eaten, but they tasted so heavenly that I couldn't stop. Once we had eaten, they looked around, and asked how I had gotten here. I told them the truth; that I had flown over the ocean and landed here. They laughed, and I let them know that I could use a ride somewhere when they were done catching more lobster. I told them that I would love to go to Chichen Itza, that there was someone I was hoping to meet there. I didn't tell them that *someone* happened to be a bird. I was sure that if I waited long enough, I would see another hummingbird there, and turn back again. Besides, what was Chichen Itza?

They agreed to take me there after more lobster catching, and it seemed to me that the aching in my body was subsiding a little by walking around. After all, I hadn't used my legs for anything but perching for the last couple of weeks. We walked down the beach a little more, and came upon some more large rocks. We caught about 20 more lobster total. Rather than eating them, we cleaned them and returned their tailless bodies to the sea. All of the tails were placed on ice in the chest.

I walked back with them to their car, getting to know them a little better. Even with the language barrier, I found out that they worked for a seafood restaurant near Chichen Itza, and that they came out to find Rock Lobster most every day in different places. What a fun job, I thought. We got back to their vehicle, an old blue Toyota four-wheel drive with no top, two normal seats up front, and two bench seats facing each other on the sides of the back. It was past its prime, but looked like a lot of fun.

We tore down the sandy road with the radio blaring, and the men started singing along with gusto. At first, I thought the song was in Spanish because of their thick accents, but when I listened harder, I realized that it was an old Reggae Caribbean Island song in English by that dreadlock hair guy, what was his name? Oh, yeah, Bob Marley. My Dad used to sing it around the house when we came to the island. It was about not worrying, and that everything would be all right. Somehow, it made me feel better. I joined in, glad that the music happened to be in English, and we had a great time singing along at the top of our lungs on the Yucatan Peninsula, driving past palm trees toward a place called Chichen Itza. Oh, if my family could see me now!

XI. Chichen Itza

As we drove into the forest, it became thicker and thicker, and soon we were in what unmistakably was jungle. Occasionally, I would notice a toucan or another brightly colored bird that I had never seen anywhere in the United States. The jungle was beautiful, but I wondered what dangerous things lived here as well. We came to several places in the road where creeks crossed it, and rather than having bridges, I just saw the road continue on the other side. The first one came on us suddenly after rounding a curve, and I expected Pedro to slow down. No such luck. He accelerated shouting, "WOOO-HOOO!!!", and drove straight through it with the pedal to the metal. Water flew up on both sides of the vehicle about 15 feet high, and we got a little shower, which was fine with me on this hot day. The sun and warm wind dried us off quickly, and we continued on our way. After driving for a while, we came to a quaint little village called Pisté.

The buildings were small, the largest being a two story hotel. They were made of either blocks or stucco, with metal or thatched roofs. The nicer ones had walls painted with bright colors. All of the structures had metal bars over the windows, and a separate metal gate instead of a screened door. It had one main street going down the middle of town, and packs of dogs around different places. It reminded me of a town from one of those old western movies that my Grandpa likes to watch. I had never been to a real Mexican town, and was having the time of my life. We passed a very old looking church with a cross on the top built of stone and stucco, and every now and then, we would see animals in the road. We saw lots of animals running around free; dogs, cats, goats, sheep, and even a pig once crossed our path.

We came to a small restaurant that had a big "Langosta" sign out front, drove around to the back and parked. Pedro honked the horn to the rhythm of *shave and a haircut, two bits*. Pretty soon, an attractive young woman in a white dress came to the door, and looked out through the barred gate. Pedro gave her a winning smile, and motioned as if he wanted to come in. I wondered what I was getting into the middle of. She disappeared, and soon out came a large, older Mexican man with balding grey hair wearing an apron. He was sweaty from working, and began to scream at Pedro in Spanish. Pedro just sat and took it with a smile, and with his eyes still fixed on the old man, turned to Enrique, who handed him the ice chest. As this man continued to shout getting redder in the face all the time, Pedro opened the chest silently and motioned his hand over it like a magician, giving a sly smile.

The man's face changed suddenly, his expression shifting from anger to almost awe. He smiled briskly, and became very friendly. He asked us all to come in, put his arm around me, and said something that I couldn't understand. I responded with, "¿Hablas inglés?"

He just laughed. "Yes. I can talk some English," He said. "Are you the reason for this good catch?"

I wasn't sure how to respond, but saw Pedro out of the corner of my eye giving a slight nod. "No," I said. "To tell you the truth, it was Pedro who taught me. I have never caught lobster before today."

"He gave us luck," Pedro said to the man, who looked at him skeptically.

He gave Pedro some money for the lobster tails, and Pedro smiled at the young woman. She smiled back and gave him a note, and we left.

We got back to the little truck, and Pedro gave me some of the money. "What's this for?" I asked. Pedro was reading the note, and was in his own little world.

"Excuse me," I said a little louder. "What's the money for?" I held it up and shrugged my shoulders with palms up and put a questioning look on my face.

Pedro broke out of his stupor and said, "Help today. Thanks!"

"I can't take this. You helped me more than I helped you," I said. But he just held his hand palm out to me in a gesture that let me know he wouldn't take it back from me. "Muchas Gracias!"

I said, not knowing what else to do, and put it in my pocket.

"Now, ju want to go to Chichen Itza?" he asked.

"Yes!" I said, still wondering what it was. It had to be interesting, or these guys wouldn't keep talking about it.

We got back into the four-wheel drive, and started off down the road. On the way, they asked me where I was spending the night.

"With some friends that I meet at Chichen Itza, as long as they are there" I said uneasily. Quickly changing the subject, I asked them what they knew about Chichen Itza. I wanted to learn about it.

"It is a—how ju say—beautiful Maya place. Been here long time." Enrique said, chiming in, speaking English to me for the first time.

"Wait. You speak English, too?" I said. I had thought that Pedro was the only one who could understand me.

"Jes. A little. I learned in school, and some at the food place," Enrique said.

"Ah, the restaurant," I said.

"Jes, the restaurant," he said.

"That's great! So, how long has Chichen Itza been around?" I asked.

"Over a thousand years" he said.

"A thousand years?!" I exclaimed. "My country hasn't been around much more than two hundred."

"Jes. You need to learn about—how ju say—ancient places," He said.

"Wow. Ancient places. Where did you learn those words?" I asked.

"From a tour guide at Chichen Itza. She say it's been there since about the year 700." He said, smiling as if proud of himself.

We pulled up to the entrance and parked. As we walked in, I kept my eyes peeled for different kinds of birds, especially small ones with a red splotch on their throat that liked nectar and hummed when they flew. The guard at the entrance recognized the three men with me, and let them pass without asking for the admission charge. Me, however, he asked for full price. I took out the money, and began to pay him, when Pedro stepped up to the man and said some things in Spanish to him. After a brief exchange, he told me that I could enter for half price. That was okay with me. I hoped I wouldn't need money for what I was going to be doing soon anyway.

We walked around a grove of trees, and it opened up into a wide, well-kept grassy area with huge ancient buildings all around. I had never seen or even imagined anything like it! Everywhere I looked there were ancient buildings made of stone as far as I could see. I thought that anything this old had to be in Egypt, Greece, or Rome, or somewhere like that. Yet here I was in Mexico, staring at ruins with pillars, a big building with what looked like an astronomy tower, and a huge *pyramid*! Was I lost? I thought the pyramids were in Egypt. But when I looked again, I noticed that they were built differently than the famous Egyptian pyramid pictures I was used to seeing.

I wanted to go over to the large pyramid right away, but Pedro, José, and Enrique pointed me in the direction of the English tour guide. Surprisingly, they wanted to come with me on the tour, telling me they could learn more English. I was pleased to have the only people I knew, even a little bit, with me here. I wondered how many times they had been here with people before. At the same time, I needed to get to a place where I could see a hummingbird, and preferably not be seen by others in the process, even my new friends. This might be tougher than I thought.

There were tour guides offering tours in different languages, and we made our way to the one in English. The tour guide began talking about the builders of the city, the Mayan people. Once, as many as 20 million Mayans lived in Central America, and this was just one of their huge cities for 100,000 plus people that they built. The thing was, by the 1400s they had abandoned all of them. Why? It was fascinating as she talked about their knowledge of astronomy, mathematics, architecture, art, and something we take for granted today, the calendar. They developed seventeen different types of calendars, including the solar one that we use now.

A large observatory stood on top of one of their buildings where they charted the planets a thousand years ago, and you could still see its crumbling roof. Once again, it was one thing to read about this stuff in books or on the computer, but completely another to be standing on the same stones as people that had stood there over a thousand years ago. And then I saw it, what I had been looking for all along. Over by a bathroom area there was a little section with bird feeders, including three hummingbird feeders. Unfortunately, no birds were there now except a greedy parrot of some kind hastily eating sunflower seeds at one of the larger feeders, but I knew that the biggest feeding time was right before bedtime, and I would be back. I looked at the sun, and decided that I had plenty of time to look at the ruins and come back, as long as I didn't get slowed down by my new friends.

We continued on the tour, and the guide showed us faces in the walls that looked different depending on the shadows of the sun, and then she said something that really stuck with me. They built all of this *without metal tools*! How could this be done? I marveled at the ingenuity of the people.

We then moved on to a rectangular ball court where they played a game where you had to get a 12-pound rubber ball through a small hoop in the side, kind of like our game of basketball, except that the grassy field was *much* bigger than a basketball court, and the hoop was vertical instead of horizontal. It had stone walls on the two longer sides of the field that held each hoop. But what struck me most was the sound of the place. It was extraordinary! José got my attention, had me stand in a corner of the field, then he ran over to the near side of the court and spoke to me in a normal tone of voice, smiling saying, "Can you hear me, now?" I laughed at his joke and for a moment was worried that I had changed back into a bird, because I could easily hear every word that he said, but when I looked up he was 200 feet away! He did it again at the far side, and although he was 500 feet away, I could hear him just as clearly as could be. I checked my feet again to make sure that I hadn't changed into a bird. Thankfully, just my feet in my shoes were there.

After seeing most of the other buildings, we finally made our way to the place I had wanted to go the whole time, the large Pyramid, *El Castillo,* or in English, *The Castle.* Towering 90 feet high, the guide said that it was positioned exactly so that twice a year on the equinoxes, a shadow would form along one side of the stairs, creating the image of a serpent, the head of which was carved at the base of the steps. If it had been built just one foot off in any other direction, this could not happen.

I asked the tour guide what an equinox was, feeling a little embarrassed, but wanting to know. She said that it was those two days a year when the length of the day is exactly the same as the length of the night. I asked when it happened in the fall, and when it happened in the spring, and she told me that it had happened about a month ago for the fall, and wouldn't happen until the third week in March for the spring equinox. I wondered when hummingbirds migrated back to the north, and if I could see it on my way back.

I was amazed at how precise the people were that built this city. Everywhere I looked, there was organization and order. She drew our attention to the steps that I couldn't wait to climb, and said that there were 91 on each side, one for every day of the year totaling 364, with the top platform representing the 365th day. I was dumbfounded. At the conclusion of the tour, the guide accepted some money for tips, including a large one from me, as I had learned so much about this area of the world from her.

We then climbed the pyramid to the top, my muscles aching all the way, and Enrique produced a camera to take a picture of us all at the top of *El Castillo*. He set the camera to timer mode, and took a shot of us all there. I told him I wanted a copy, and gave him my email address.

"Do ju see the people ju are going to meet?" Pedro asked.

"No," I said. "I think I know where they will be now, though."

By now it was much later in the day, and I was sure that there would be some birds at the feeders. As much as I was enjoying time with my new friends, I was anxious to get on with my journey. I needed to turn back into a hummingbird again. How could I accomplish this without anyone knowing? We went back toward the bathrooms, and much to my chagrin, there were no ruby-throats. They didn't seem too surprised that I would be meeting people here as it was a pretty common meeting place.

"They're not here," I said, and walked over by the hummingbird feeders and acted like I was killing time waiting for someone. They waited patiently with me, and when it was within an hour of dark, I was really starting to get worried. Where could they be?

"Ju like the colibrí?" Enrique said, pointing to the hummingbird feeder. I nodded. After we had waited for a little while, they wanted to get home.

"Come back and have some food with us," José said. After all that they had done for me, I felt guilty not going, and we left. Bouncing along the road wasn't nearly as fun as it had been earlier today when I thought I would get to see some hummingbirds and continue my promised journey. Instead, I was beginning to be a bit concerned. Where would I sleep, how long would I have to wait? Here I was in a foreign country and although I now had some friends, I felt very much alone.

We reached the restaurant again, ordered some burritos and my personal favorite, Chimichanga with rice and we began to eat. The young woman in the white dress that we had seen earlier waited on us, and Enrique and José were constantly making fun of Pedro because of his flirtation with her. After the meal, we all left and went for a walk in the twilight air. I stopped on the road after a bit, noticing a map in a shop window of Central America, blown up. I looked it over as thoroughly as I could, noting the location of different countries, because I wasn't sure where I would be flying next. Come to think of it, I wasn't sure *if* I would be flying again. We passed by a small spot of grass where some boys were playing soccer. José joined in for a little bit, and then we resumed our walk. They took me into a really neat old brown stucco building with columns and a large porch on the second floor overlooking the restaurant with flowers of all kinds growing along its railings, and buzzing around it there they were: all kinds of hummingbirds.

I stood in wonder at these creatures, even more inspired because I had spent time actually living as one. Now, all I had to do was to somehow get back up here alone, because I didn't want these guys to see me change into a bird. Come to think of it, would the Binoculars even work if someone was watching me? I had been alone before when I changed into a hummingbird the first time, and I wasn't willing to take the chance of being seen now. I made a lame excuse that I needed to find some way to meet my friends, and that I really needed to leave tonight. I told them not to worry if they didn't see me again, because if I saw who I needed to see, I would have to leave immediately. They looked at me strangely, but seemed to understand what I was saying, and we all went downstairs. As we were going down the steps on a landing, the young woman from the restaurant came up, and Pedro blurted out, "Carmen!" when he saw her. She made a motion that she wanted to see Pedro upstairs on the veranda. He looked at me and made a quick motion to keep going down with the other two, and I saw my chance. I nodded to him.

Immediately, I asked Enrique and José what kind of fish they liked to catch in the ocean other than lobsters. Not a very good question, but it did the job of distracting them and we continued walking. They started talking about fishing, and pretty soon there was a "one that got away" story as we walked along. I made an excuse that I needed to go to the bathroom, remembering that there was one on the bottom floor of the old stucco building with the veranda. I turned back, and walked briskly to it. My plan was that they would wait there while I went back alone. It didn't work. They followed me, saying that they needed to go, too. I got there first, realized it was a one holer, and went in. When I came out, Enrique went in, and José was waiting. I gave a wry smile and acted as if I were spying on Pedro, motioned for José to stay there, and headed up the stairs to a room with large half-circle shaped openings with white see-through curtains that looked out onto the veranda. There were no lights on in the room, so I could still see out without them seeing in. I really didn't have any desire to see Pedro and Carmen together, but it was a good excuse to get to a place alone to see the hummingbirds and change back so I could continue my journey.

Pedro and Carmen were in a deep discussion, voices low, and heads very close together. He reached up and put his hands on her cheeks as if to kiss her when I thought I saw a ruby-throated hummingbird come by and perch on a flower stem. I moved my head quickly to get a better look at it, and hit a hanging flower pot just above my head, causing a loud bang. It hurt, but I needed to get changed quickly. I saw Pedro turn around at the sound, and heard him mutter something about

Enrique and José. Then, I heard footsteps coming up the stairs. The hummingbird was perched on a little branch in front of a flower. It was now or never. I tried to remember the exact words I had said before, put the Binoculars to my eyes and muttered softly aloud, "I wonder where you go, little one. I'd love to go with you, and find out."

Nothing. Pedro kept coming towards the room where I was. I could hear that he was almost at the door! The footsteps on the stairs were getting closer. I hadn't lined it up right! Lining the line up with the bird, I looked through the Binoculars and repeated the phrase. Just as Pedro opened the door, he saw Enrique, who was pointing and laughing at him, and Pedro was angry, but he didn't want to lose his cool with Carmen nearby. He began speaking very pointedly in firm but not loud speech with his jaw clenched. The words were something in Spanish to the effect of, "Enrique, get out of here." Neither of them seemed to notice a little hummingbird that had just materialized in the room from a boy. I thought it was getting a bit tense between these two friends, so I flew nose to nose with each of them for a brief moment, hummed around both of their heads, and then hovered in between them for a while. It wasn't long before they were laughing again at the situation. It's amazing the effect a little bird can have on people.

This having been accomplished, I flew out of one of the semicircle shaped openings to the veranda where Carmen was waiting, and flew right up and hovered in front of her face for a few seconds. I could see why Pedro liked her. After that, I flew to the flowers and began drinking the nectar. Another hummer came up, and I dive bombed him a couple of times until he left. I sat perched, drinking in the rich nectar. They gathered around me, staring. By now José had made it to the top of the stairs and out onto the veranda, and stood by them, just staring. I couldn't understand what they were saying, as they spoke very quickly in Spanish, but it seemed to be of confusion, not of awareness as if someone saw me change. I was relieved by that. Although I regretted having to leave my new friends, I knew that they would somehow understand, and that it would be all right. They watched me as I flew away, going as high as I could and then, in one last long dive for their benefit, I pulled out of it and was gone.

I found refuge in a secluded spot, a nearby tree with some gnarled branches wrapped around the trunk and stretching out in every direction. Although I was full from having eaten a lot that day, I was still underweight, and exhausted. I can't remember ever being so tired in all of my life. I put my head back, and began sleeping almost immediately, again with my bill straight up.

XII. On to the Unknown

I awoke in the middle of the night to a sudden awareness of danger. Not understanding it, I shivered my wings for a few seconds before seeing movement in the form of a shadow along the branch. *Something was coming into the branches here.* It was not walking, but wrapped around the branch itself, with a part of its body coiled up on the top not far from me. A snake! The gnarled branches that surrounded me could do nothing to keep a snake out. Instead, they were acting as a cage to keep me in! As a boy, I might be curious as to what kind of snake it was, but in that moment, I didn't have time to think of anything but escape. Besides, it didn't matter if it was poisonous or not if I was about to be eaten in one gulp.

I kept my head in the same position, pointed straight up to keep it thinking I was still asleep, opened my eyes halfway and saw that it was clear directly above, and I took off, shooting straight up and out, just as the snake's mouth came down on the branch below where I had just been perched. I managed to make it to another tree without any strange shadowy shapes around, and this time, I was shivering from fear. So that was something else to look out for as a bird. Only my bird instinct had saved me! It took a while to calm down enough to actually get back to sleep, but in the end, exhaustion won and I fell asleep amid the shelter of another tree.

When I awoke, it was just before sunrise. Now, where to? According to the map in the window, the country due South of where I was on the Yucatan Peninsula was Belize, and then over a little more water in the Gulf, then on to Honduras. I knew nothing of Belize, and only a little about Honduras because my Dad had been there once. From there, where did I go and for how long? I hoped that the path would become clearer as I went. I finished the night's sleep without incident, and in the morning began my normal routine of finding the right food in the jungle. I wanted to go back to Chichen Itza and fly around in some of the buildings that tourists weren't allowed in, also hoping to hang out near the feeders and see a hummingbird there to follow. If not, there was always the veranda here in Pisté to find some.

I headed along the tops of the trees that ran right along the road to Chichen Itza, and it wasn't long before I could see the ruined buildings towering over the trees of the jungle. I went into some of the doors that were closed to tourists, and saw some hieroglyphic writing that told a story about a prince and a princess marrying, or at least that's what I think it was about. Parts of the walls the story was written on were broken. Others I saw, too, that were not as pleasant. I flew back to the feeder area and perched for a long drink. At the very least, the free nectar at the feeders was very welcome on this hot day, and I knew that I could only stay a day or two recovering from my flight over the ocean before I had to move on.

An uneventful and restful night followed, and I resumed my watch for a ruby-throat. The next day I saw another hummingbird, and, keeping at a distance, followed him for a while. Although my wings were still tired from the long flight over the Gulf of Mexico just days earlier, they no longer ached, and I could feel that they were actually stronger. It wasn't difficult to keep up, and I stayed far enough away that I hoped I wouldn't be a nuisance to him.

He was leaving Chichen Itza, and we flew just over the trees about 200 feet apart, headed due south. Every so often, he would find some flowers, and I would look for some as well, or just wait in the tree tops until he continued flying again. We had flown a good way when he went down, I assumed to find some food, and I found some really good nectar and had a longer than usual drink, thinking that I needed it for a flight of unknown length. I then returned to the tree top, and couldn't see him anywhere. I waited for what seemed like ages, and no bird. I had to continue on. Great, now I was on my own again! I continued flying, and after several miles, I heard his distinct hum behind me. He had waited me out, and was now following me. I figured that if I went the wrong way, he would correct the course and I could again follow him. But he just stayed behind me for mile after mile, so I felt pretty good that I was going the right way, wherever that was.

The jungle below me was beautiful, and I saw lots of interesting sights along the way; toucans in flight, brightly colored woodpeckers, and a cuckoo that I only recognized because of its call. Other types I would have to look up online or in a book when I got home, *if* I got home. Occasionally, I would come across a boa constrictor or other snake slithering around. I seemed to see a lot of them, and wondered if it was due to my vision as a hummingbird or if it was because there were so many of them. Either way, I was glad to be in the air. I have never had a fondness for snakes, but that incident in the tree had made me absolutely loathe them now.

We flew over towns, and one pretty good-sized city where there were parks with bird houses, and usually there were hummingbird feeders. These really helped, as it saved moving so much from flower to flower and wasting all of that time. They were like little gas stations for us hummingbirds. At one stop, I noticed that the bird that I had started following and was now following me had stopped for a drink as well. I decided to speak to him.

"Where are you headed?" I asked.

"I was going to ask you the same thing. Aren't we both going to the other coast, or do you stop sooner?" he asked. So that's where hummingbirds go when they migrate! I decided agreement was the best thing.

"That's where I'm headed, but this is my first trip. I'm not quite sure of the way." I said.

"Your first trip! You're a juvenile? You look full grown. You should have stayed back, and come after the females," He said.

"I wanted to get here and stake out my territory first. It's important to me," I said, trying to cover. He looked at me doubtfully, and then said that I still should have waited.

We finished with our nectar, and he hummed off, higher than before. I followed, and he turned and began dive bombing me. I returned the favor, and soon we were having an aerial battle high above the trees. Other birds came and watched, and in the end, I drove him away. He came back and hummed right in front of my nose and said, "You'll make it. We can go together, but not very far, and only for a day, if that. Keep at least the distance we were keeping before. I'll lead." And with that, he flew off.

I followed, and soon we came to water again. Here was another coast. Was this where we would spend the winter? He flew higher, and I knew that we were flying over it. Maybe on the other side of the water, I hoped. We both flew up pretty high and then descended slowly, flying about 20 feet over the surface. The water was as beautiful as any I had ever seen. I could see all the way to the bottom, and occasionally my eyes could spy some Rock Lobster walking along. I wondered if Pedro, Enrique, and José ever came this far to find *Langosta*. Soon we were over land again, and we stopped to find more nectar. There were some fisherman on the beach catching some good fish, and I wished I could say hello to them.

We continued on, and pretty soon, the terrain changed and we were over mountains. It was beautiful, with many streams and trees. There were flowers everywhere, and I saw wild parrots and macaws out flying in flocks. They were huge to me as a hummingbird and I kept my distance, but admired them anyway. I was tired in the afternoon, as we had to climb continually to get over these mountains. Every so often, I would see a grouping of small trees organized like an orchard, and wondered what kind it was, but I didn't dare leave my leader through the mountains. We used a pass, and at the highest part of it, rain began to fall. We flew for a little while, but it wasn't long before it was such a hard rain that I couldn't see the other bird. I went down into the tree tops, and found a little shelter under a large leaf. I was tired and it looked like the rain may be coming down for a while, so I checked the area over to be sure it was safe, and fell asleep.

The rain was over when I awoke, and I tried to find my dive bombing friend. With no luck after a few minutes, I knew it was time to move on. If he wanted to travel together, I guessed he would find me. I flew up to the top of the trees to look for him, and couldn't believe the beauty of what was before me. After the rain, there were waterfalls all over the mountains, and I just watched, taking it all in. I had seen waterfalls before, but never this many at one time, and with such long drops! There were low lying clouds in the valley, and I felt on top of the world being above the clouds like this. I really didn't mind being alone if it was going to be this beautiful.

On the way back down the mountain I flew through some of the closer waterfalls for a good bath. It felt great! After a few more hours, I stopped to take a break in a garden of flowers that smelled particularly good. I was up in the treetop level, and came upon a family of monkeys all playing tag, or so it looked. They were having a great time, and could go from branch to branch as easily as I could fly. I perched watching the monkeys, enjoying the time. They were graceful, and seemed to have fun.

I continued flying until almost sundown, and figured that the mountain crossing was enough for me today. I hoped that there weren't any more. I tried to remember the map from the store window, and was sure that I was in the southern part of Honduras right now. I would continue south, pass through Nicaragua, and if I stayed straight south, would make it to Costa Rica sometime tomorrow. If I was really headed to "the other coast", and was to continue south, that was most likely my destination. I hoped that it wasn't any further than that. I could hardly believe all of this was happening to me. Just weeks ago, I had never been anywhere but home and Seabird Island.

I fueled up on nectar and found a seemingly safe place to sleep. There seemed to be power lines nearby, something I thought a bit odd in the treetops on the side of a mountain. I guessed that the people here needed electricity just like people anywhere else.

I was awakened in the morning by some familiar but strange noises. I went down just a little bit to investigate, and heard a noise that sounded like something scraping against metal, and fast. Pretty soon, I noticed that what I had thought were power lines were shaking, and not long after that, a person came down in a harness with a pulley attached to one line and safety chain attached to the other, shouting as if he were having a lot of fun. When he got down, he called back up to someone else, and the sliding sound began again with another person coming down on a pulley system hooked to a harness and safety chain. I looked, and what I thought had been power lines were actually big zip lines, and coming down one by one were people. Eventually, there were four of them standing on a wooden platform near the tops of the trees. I got closer and listened to them.

"This is great!" I heard a woman say. "So this is the treetop canopy. Are there any interesting birds here?"

"Look over there," a darker man said with a Spanish accent. He pointed directly at me. She looked.

"That's a hummingbird!" She said. "We have them back home in Boston. I was hoping for something a little more exotic."

"They are amazing creatures, the hummingbirds, and aren't easy to find. I have never seen this one before. You should enjoy it while you can," he said, and watched me with his own binoculars, as if I were fascinating to him. I put on a little bit of an aerial show, and flew closer to them. I flew upside-down in front of the whole group, and landed on the woman's shoulder. She said, "Wow! He's wonderful!"

Satisfied, I knew that I needed to find food and fly on. I flew off, and heard exclamations from them about other creatures in the canopy as I left. Maybe they saw something more exotic than me. I found some brilliantly colored flowers with good nectar, drank my fill, and went on my way.

It wasn't long before I saw what had to be another orchard of the same type I had seen before, planted on the steepest part of the mountain. It was made up of perfectly-spaced trees, and planted over a small section of ground growing almost straight up. Curious, I went down and flew around them to see what they could be. The leaves were small and dark green, and there were what looked like some kind of red berries all over each of them. Then I smelled it, and it was unmistakable: coffee. These were coffee farms, and I had been seeing them all over. None were very big, not at all like the massive fields of corn or soybean farms seen in the United States, but there were a lot of them dotting the landscape of the mountains. I left the coffee grove, went on my way south, and decided to fly until I had reached my destination, if possible. I hoped it would be obvious to me. It was impossible to tell when I crossed over the boundary of Honduras and Nicaragua, as there aren't any boundary lines in the sky. Somehow, I wondered if that was how we were supposed to live.

I kept going south, and could always tell direction by the location of the sun, even when it was directly overhead. I flew as fast as possible, only stopping for food, enjoying the beauty of many more things along the way. There were more mountains, but after the first ones in Honduras, I knew how to handle them, and could always find a pass to fly over. I saw an immense lake after most of the day, and knew I had to be in southern Nicaragua, near the border to Costa Rica. I had seen it on the map. While flying over the mountains in what I was sure now was Costa Rica, I saw a large stream of thick, dense smoke ascending from the top of one of the mountains. I wanted to go and check it out, but I was focused on getting to the end of my journey, so that would have to wait for now. At the end of this day, I saw far off the coast of the Pacific Ocean. Hopefully, this was my destination, my home away from the winter up north.

XIII. Costa Rica

After a good night's sleep and fresh nectar, I planned on finding some other hummingbirds, if possible. Flying alone was one thing, but being away from my family, I wanted to have some friends during however long I was going to be here. I had made one, sort of, but didn't know what had happened to him along the way. I hoped that he was all right.

I started by looking for feeders in the numerous people settlements just inland from the beach. Many had hummingbird feeders, and I enjoyed those a lot. Pretty soon, I began to see other hummers. I routinely had to fight off other males for food, but didn't mind it, figuring I had to prove myself. One day, I was fighting off two ruby-throats when a couple more showed up, and were trying to take me on all at once. With the odds four against one, I was just barely holding my own. Then another one came in, and I was sure I was going to have to leave the territory. Wait, I recognized this last hummer by the sound of his wing beats, and instead of coming to fight against me he began fighting side by side with me. I had found him, the one I had traveled with and had helped show me the way here.

"I see you made it," he said between dive bombs.

"What happened to you? I lost you in the rain," I asked with a sudden duck and hover maneuver I had practiced in the woods back on the island.

"I had a run-in with some monkeys when I tried to find cover in that rainstorm. They wanted to play with me, and that can be deadly, so I flew away," he said. By this time, our attackers had had enough, and flew away one by one.

"After that, I didn't want to wait in case there was another hidden danger there, and flew through the rain until I found a place to sleep. I figured you would be all right. We all make this journey alone, after all," he said.

"When is the rest of your family going to get here?" he asked.

I didn't know what to say. I had never expected to have to explain myself to a hummingbird.

"What do you mean?" I asked.

"You know, the rest of your family. You are a juvenile, so your Dad should be here already, then your Mom, and then your brothers and sisters. You may not see them much, but they should be here," he said.

I looked at him sadly because I missed my real family. I couldn't begin to tell him my story, so I just said that they couldn't come.

"Cheer up. You can be the brother I never had while you're here. Mine died when I was a juvenile, and I've always wanted one. What's your name?" he asked.

"Ben," I said.

"Well, Ben, I'm Chan," he said.

"Good to meet you, Chan," I said.

"You know, you've got to teach me that ducking thing that you do," he said.

"It's easy. It'll take you maybe a half-hour of practice. Can you teach me some things?" I asked.

"Like what?" he asked.

"Like what you do down here all winter," I said.

"The most important thing we've just done, proving ourselves for our territory. Every now and then, we will have to defend it, but from here on out, it will be ours. It's in the same territory I have had for the past several years, this area of people dwellings," he said. "The rest of my family will be down in the next couple of weeks, and we will share it with them, as well as some of the local birds."

As if on cue, some of the local hummingbirds flew down to the feeders, feathered in all of the colors of the rainbow. They were larger than we were, so we flew out of their way and waited our turn. My favorite was an iridescent blue one that seemed to sparkle when he flew. I had taken enough nectar for now, and as I hovered out of the way, I watched them with awe. Even though I was a hummingbird right now myself, I still couldn't believe how gorgeous these creatures were. I discovered in that moment that the best way to be a bird watcher was to be a bird yourself. I was inches away from them, and of course they weren't scared at all. On the contrary, I got the feeling that they were glad we were there. I asked Chan if there were other interesting birds down here, and he seemed surprised by my question.

"Yes, if you like very brightly colored birds. I think that they are gaudy myself. I think that a bird should have just enough color to get the attention of his mate; anything more is just too much. That's not always a good thing, because the ability to hide is crucial anywhere you go," Chan said.

"Well, the flowers and trees are so much more brightly colored here. Shouldn't the birds be able to hide better if they are brightly colored?" I asked.

"Yes. You're catching on. There are some really nice green birds that match the color of our backs and have a red chest kind of like us, but the entire chest is red instead of just the throat and they are much bigger than we are. They are hard to spot because they stay in green trees, but if you ever see one flying, you will be glad you did. Their long tail feathers trail out behind them, and they are a beautiful sight," he said. Later that day he pointed one out to me and there were people around. They called it a "quetzal."

"I'd love to see different kinds of birds with you and your family this winter," I said.

"You can, and you can teach my juveniles how to duck and hover," he said.

"How many do you have?" I asked.

"Two," he said. "A male and a female."

"That's just like my—" I trailed off. I was going to say that's just like my sister and me, but again, I didn't want to have to explain myself.

"Just like what?" he asked.

"It's just like my family was. I miss them," I said.

"That's all right. You can be a part of ours, now," he said.

"Thanks!" I said, brightening.

"Where is your home up north?" I asked. I wanted to know how far he had flown.

"It's a long flight through a mixture of trees and high hard walled places with lots of those colorful wheeled boxes traveling on the ground to look at," he said. "It's a fun flight, not far from the ocean most of the way." So he had to travel through cities on his way down. That probably meant he was on the Eastern seaboard.

"How far north do you live, then?" I asked. Then I took a chance and said, "Have you ever heard any of the people say the name of the place?"

"I think that people call it something like New Brunslick," he replied. "I'm not sure."

Wow, he must mean New Brunswick! That was way up north of Maine in Canada! I looked him over again, and was astounded that a bird as small as we were could travel so far year after year.

"How long do you stay down here?" I asked.

"Until it's time to go. It's usually about 100 downs and ups of the big eye in the sky," he said.

Ah, so just over three months we would be down here. Wait, plus the two and a half weeks I had already spent in preparation and the journey, that totaled four months. Four months? Grandpa said that he would help me cover the time, but how was he going to cover four months? My family would be worried sick, refusing to go back home, and have all kinds of people looking for me! The ramifications of that amount of time scared me. Surely they would think that I was dead. If it weren't for Grandpa's insistence not to worry about time, I would have flown back right now and changed back to a boy. As it was, though, I knew that I should stay and build up my strength and weight. By the time I did that, it would be too cold up there to survive the flight back. I guess if you're going to be stuck somewhere, a tropical paradise as a hummingbird isn't the worst you could do.

"100 days? That's a long time. I didn't know we stayed down here so long," I said.

"That's the life of a hummingbird," he said.

"What do we do here all of that time?" I asked.

"Enjoy the warmth, the length of the days, the flowers, the insects, and the feeders. You'll also see the other birds that come in from all over. It's an amazing place," he said. "Birds come from down south of here as well as from up north like we did. Just stay away from the monkeys and snakes."

"Do you make a nest down here to live in?" I asked.

"No. We have our young up north. We don't build a nest unless we are having young," he said. "I usually don't travel around much while I'm here. I stay pretty much around this territory."

"Would it bother you if I traveled some while I am here? I am fascinated by this new country," I said.

"You can go anytime you want to, but remember, you are crossing over many other bird's territories when you do, and not all of them like that very much," he said.

Over the next few weeks, Chan's lady, Ann, made her way there, and it wasn't long before his two young ones, Dan and Jan made it down. I was glad that there were several feeders here, or it could have been interesting in the morning and evening feeding times with all of us and the local hummers here, too. The people who had put the feeders out loved us buzzing around their heads, and I found great joy in spending my days in a routine of feeding in the morning with the other hummers, hiding in a safe spot in the trees, and then feeding in the evening again, but after a month of this, the boy side of me grew restless.

One morning, I heard a loud growling sound a fair distance away that was answered by a similar sound even farther away. I looked to see if I could figure out what it was, but couldn't find anything out of the ordinary. I decided to go and explore some on my own, and flew up one of the mountains that separated the East and West Sides of Costa Rica. During a late afternoon, I was looking for food when I noticed a line of my favorite nectar flowers across a field. There was something dark between me and the flowers that looked kind of like a spider web, but I took no notice as flying through spider webs was no big deal, and sometimes I got to eat a spider from it. Flying directly towards the flowers, when I got about ten feet away from the nectar I stopped flying abruptly and could no longer move. My head turned to the left side, my feet were caught, and if I struggled, I was caught more. This was no spider web, I was in a net! Who would put up a net here and why?

I stopped struggling because that just made it worse and thankfully, a man who was watching the nets soon came and took me out of the net and placed me in a mesh bag about the size of a sandwich bag with a drawstring at the top. He cinched the drawstring, and I was tempted to change back into a boy and give him a real scare, but decided against it. This man was most likely a scientist of some kind. Besides, I didn't want the publicity of a boy who could change into a hummingbird, and I sure didn't want anyone taking my magnificent Binoculars away. He picked up some other birds along the way and placed them in bags as well on his way to a little tent with a table in it with all sorts of gear. He hung the bird bags on a spindle, and turned it slowly to retrieve the bags one at a time.

When it came to my turn, he carefully removed the bag I was in, and held onto me very firmly with my head between his middle and index fingers, my feathered body in his hand. Surprisingly, it didn't hurt at all. It was obvious that he meant no harm, and had done this with many birds. He placed a smaller bag over me and placed me on a scale, muttering aloud to himself about my weight. A small laptop was there, and he typed in some information about me. He then took me over to an open box that scared me at first because it looked like a big fishing tackle box with lots of metal and different sizes of pliers in it. What could he be doing? I struggled to get out of his grip, but found that I couldn't move.

He took out a little metal ring with writing on it, held out my foot, and placed the ring around my leg. After that, he reached into the tackle box and grabbed some pliers that didn't quite come together, and clamped the ring around my leg. I was banded! I remembered that scientists do this in order to track birds' migration paths, but wasn't sure how this would affect me. Could I change back with this thing on my leg? Would it simply come off, would it give me a cut, or even worse, cut off my leg? I didn't want to find out. It didn't weigh much, but I knew that I would feel even that little weight on my long flight back over the water.

I couldn't worry about it much now as it was done, and when the man let me go, I happily flew over the net to the flowers and had my fill of nectar. I thought the band might affect my balance, but the weight change was hardly noticeable.

Continuing on up the mountain, I saw many beautiful birds as well as monkeys, jaguars, and waterfalls with little pools, just like in the movies! These I flew through for a bath, and saw piles of stones that were evidence that ancient people had once lived there. I was traveling from the south up a tall mountain filled with green trees, and everything in the air suddenly felt different. It was warmer, and not from thermals. It was as if the ground itself was getting hot. Steam came up from holes in the earth every so often, kind of like pictures that I had seen of Yellowstone Park. What was going on? Then, I reached the very top and flew over a rise and everything was clear; I was on the top of a volcano. A real, active volcano!

Stretched out before me along the entire north side of the mountain was a large bowl of steaming land with a strangely colored lake in the middle of it. The water of the lake was sort of a milky blue-green. I flew high over the bowl to it, and when I reached the lake, I flew lower and could tell that the water was very warm, maybe even boiling. I saw the same kind of smoke beginning to billow up from it that I had seen on my flight down, and remembered that I had wanted to check it out before. I decided to investigate at a higher altitude, so I flew up higher for a panoramic view. Then it happened.

I felt the air getting warmer, and instinctively flew higher and higher, riding these sudden thermals created by the earth below me. I wanted to get to the trees, but as I turned to speed that way, suddenly the air all around me was filled with smoke, and solid objects were flying up all around me. I looked down, and what I had thought were solid rocks were breaking open on the ground below me like water balloons bursting. It was LAVA! One direct hit and I was a goner! I needed to get out of here, and fast! I flew as high as I could, going faster than any dive I had ever attempted in the reverse direction, and just when I thought I was safe, I hovered and looked down, only to discover another volley coming right up at me! I jetted away at the same altitude at terrifying speed, and felt the air heat up almost unbearably right where I had just been. I wasn't sure how much more of this I could take. I continued my horizontal flight, and was able to get back to the south side and go down a little bit, hiding in the cover of the green trees.

It was a long time before I moved again, slowly recovering my wits and marveling at the remarkable event that had just occurred. I couldn't move, and checking the area for predators and seeing none, decided after many hours and other eruptions from higher up that I needed to sleep. It took a while to calm down enough to get to a state where I could sleep, but eventually, I drifted off.

I awoke a few hours before dawn after a fitful sleep, and flew to the top of the tree to get a look at the light coming from the volcano. It was still dark, but I saw bright flashes every now and then, and decided to get a better look from a safe distance. I flew around the mountain this time at a higher altitude, and once I was on the northern portion, I was able to see them: streams of lava flowing like little rivers down the mountain. Deadly as they were, there was also a peaceful beauty to them as I hovered at a safe distance and altitude from their devastating heat. My eyes were drawn all the way up the mountain to the source where there were sudden vertical spouts every so often followed by the peaceful streams of glowing rock cascading down the northern side. It was a melancholy feeling to see such devastation and beauty at the same time, and I was excited and scared all at once. I flew around at a safe distance as long as I could, took it all in, and then found a safe place to rest for the remainder of the night.

After finding some particularly fine nectar on a part of the southern side of the mountain again, I came upon a path that people were walking up. I desperately wanted to get their attention and warn them not to go up, that the volcano was active, but knew that short of becoming a boy again and talking to them that there was nothing I could do. The group seemed to be following a guide, so I just left that up to him and flew on, heading back down the mountain, following the path. More people came up every so often in small groups, some with guides, some on their own. When I reached a point near the bottom, there was a sign, in English and Spanish that read *Volcan Arenal/Arenal Volcano National Park.* They had national parks in Costa Rica? Cool! I flew around the park area, and was inspired by its beauty. I decided to spend some time here in this paradise, out of reach of any lava flow.

A few days later after a good night's sleep, in the very early morning just as the flowers were opening and I was beginning to get my nectar out of them, I heard a long howling noise that sounded like it was coming from many animals. A few moments later, it seemed to be answered several miles away, and then there it was again, close by. What was this? I was curious and flew higher into the canopy, closer to where the noise had been. I saw a large family of monkeys gathered in the canopy of the trees, munching happily on the leaves up there. Their fur was black, and there were 12 large monkeys and 5 little ones, some taking piggy-back rides on their mother's back. They were remarkably agile with their prehensile tails, using them as if they had another long arm with a hand. They could hang their entire body by this incredible tail, and use their hands and feet to grab leaves and flowers that they wanted to eat. Entranced by their behavior, I flew closer to them. There was a really cute little baby monkey that I wanted to see better, so I went and hovered in front of him. He made a softer call to the others, and within moments a few of the younger ones were over on the branch all around me. I think that they wanted to play, and I remembered Chan's warning. I wished I was a boy, and could play with these little guys, but I knew that if I changed now, the adults might knock me out of the tree. From this height, that would be bad, so I decided to fly up higher, out of their reach.

I felt the air above me vibrate for an instant, and I instinctively moved to the side, but too late! I felt the body of one of the baby monkeys that had decided to go for a little tree dive crash down on top of me, and we were both plummeting down, down, down. Oh, no! What had I done? I just wanted to see them up close! As he fell, he began howling intermittently, almost as if he was laughing, and before I knew it, the other little ones all began chortling too and jumped off the limb one by one toward us. I was able to keep flapping, and through some miracle was able to get around his soft, furry body and begin to hover, only to discover four more bodies coming at me from above. I dodged them quickly, and watched them now from above as they fell, seemingly laughing all the way down. By this time, they had the full attention of the adults, who began howling and jumping down in controlled falls, limb by limb, and with amazing deftness, all reached limbs about 75 feet down perfectly safe, much to my relief. I decided not to wait and see if they would return to where I was, and knew that it was time for me to fly on. It had been a good time here at the volcano, but after a couple of weeks away, the hummingbird side of me wanted to get back to my own territory.

I traveled back and was reunited with Chan and his family. At first, they were concerned about the band on my leg. They pecked at it, trying to get it off, but in the end I didn't want them hurting their bills, so I told them that it was not a big deal. I told them stories of my adventures, and they seemed petrified that I would do the things that I did, so I didn't say anything else about my time away the rest of my time there. We spent time together, and the beauty and serenity of Costa Rica made the time pass quickly. It seemed like just a few days had passed when it was time to return.

XIV. Return Home

Chan let me know that we needed to really start preparing our bodies and minds for the trip about two weeks before our departure date. We began fattening up and going over every part of the route in our minds. One night as I was drifting off to sleep, I was amazed with what clarity I could see the images of the path home in my mind, my little bb-sized brain remembering almost every resting tree and feeder along the way. I wasn't worried about getting lost at all. I knew I could find my way. In this way, it was good to be a hummingbird.

We had both just completed a molt when the day came, and gleamed brightly in the sun. Chan and I said our goodbyes to his family, since we may never see each other again. We agreed to travel individually a few hours apart, but it wasn't very likely in that great big sky that we would see one another over the course of the trip. I left first, wanting to go as early as possible, and began long before the sun had risen over the mountain. I had lost track of the days exactly, but it was somewhere in the first week of March when I began the return flight. It was a good flight, and I made it to the Honduran Mountains before the day was out. I stopped there, refueled my tank with nectar and bugs, and went on to Chichen Itza the next day. It wasn't quite the time of the spring equinox yet, and as much as I wanted to see the shadow of the snake on the pyramid, my longing for getting back to my family was greater than my desire to see a shadow on a pyramid.

I was tempted to try to find Pedro, Enrique, and José, but I knew that they could be anywhere out along the coast searching for *Langosta*. I did go to the veranda where I had changed into a hummingbird, and got a lot of good nectar there before traveling to the trees along the coast. There, I took the most sleep that I could before the big trip north, going to sleep long before the sun went down. The next morning I awoke early ready to go, but could tell something was wrong. The pressure in my head didn't feel right, and when I began to fly out of the trees toward the shore, I noticed that the wind was from the north to the south. So, I waited for two more days until it changed, which probably was good because I was better rested and a little fatter.

On one of the days while I was waiting, I flew out along the shore and was hoping to see some rock lobster or my friends, when I again suddenly felt like I was being watched. There were two hawks coming at me from two different angles, and I wasn't sure what to do. My duck and hover maneuver wouldn't work with two of them. This time, I was too high to get down to the ground in time to change back, and didn't want to free fall over a hundred feet down as a boy. I began a dive, but the hawk dives so much faster that I knew I couldn't get away this time. As one of the hawks drew closer and got a better look at me, he let out a blood curdling screech to the other one, who seemed to answer back something I couldn't understand. Just before the first one was on me, I closed my eyes expecting the talons to tear me apart, and at that moment, I heard another screech, this time of pain, from the hawk about to dig his claws into me.

I looked up, and saw that one of the hawks had a white mark resembling a cross on his chest, and he had clawed at the other just as I was about to be lunch. The other one flew off, and the one with the cross marking flew in wide circles around me, watching all directions as if he were guarding me. Looking closer, I saw that he had a scar just below his right eye, as well as a mark on his left foot. I couldn't believe it! It was the hawk that I had helped all those months ago! He had remembered me, and had now saved my life. He must have really appreciated those fish I had given him. His flight feathers had grown back completely, and a more magnificent hawk I had never seen, scars and all! I was reminded of Grandpa's words that help would come from unexpected places, and my Dad always teaching me that good deeds would return to you. I surely never would have expected a hawk to save the life of a hummingbird, but I guess appreciation comes in all forms. From then on, each and every time I came out of the trees, he came and silently circled me, keeping me safe.

Once the wind changed, I could feel the change in the pressure in my head leading me toward the high pressure, and it was a gorgeous day on the beach. I took my last fill of nectar, and began my flight as high as I could go. The hawk with the white cross on his chest accompanied me as usual, and I went higher than I normally would have, guided by my new friend to find thermals that would lift me into the air with little effort. We were an unlikely pair, a hawk and a hummingbird, but I was thankful for his watchful eyes. I worried about nothing here with him circling around me. Then the time came for us to part, as I needed to continue on my journey over the water. Reluctantly, I said goodbye to the hawk. He nodded his head majestically, and continued ascending, flying in circles.

I decided to stay up higher this time as the winds were more favorable here, and far below me I once again saw fishing boats, bottle-nosed dolphins and the azure blue water. I let out a long, contented sigh to be in this place, but was now feeling the yearnings to get home more than ever. After all that I had seen, it was going to take me years just to process it all. Then there was a sound coming from behind me. It was the sound of other birds. Oh, no! What if there were predators in the flock? My hawk friend was long gone now, I couldn't fight off more than a couple at a time through aerial maneuvers if they came at me, and there was nowhere to hide up here! I turned and hovered for a brief moment to get a better look, and was relieved to see that they were all various kinds of songbirds, chattering to one another like crazy.

They were flying just a little faster than I had been, and I thought that maybe I could join them. They seemed to be flying in the same direction that I was, so I just stayed on course and let them overtake me. I was worried that I couldn't keep up with them, but found that I was able to stay at their speed fairly easily once I joined their flock. I stayed in the middle, and the windbreak created by all of those other birds really helped me conserve my energy while maintaining good speed all the time. We took turns being in front by large waves of birds moving forward while others retreated every so often, and after several hours it was my turn to be up there. It was all I could do to keep going and my energy really went downhill, but I knew that since I had let them make flying easier for me, I would have to take my turn and do the same for them.

We flew all day, and the wind conditions remained favorable. We made better time this trip than I had alone on the way down. There were a couple of hummers in the flock other than myself, and though we seemed to always know where the others were, we stayed apart. I again saw amazing things way down there in the water; a sperm whale surfacing, a whale shark slowly coming near the surface with its massive mouth wide open, and at one point I saw what looked like a group of submarines under the water in formation, but I couldn't stop or even slow down to find out for sure. I had to keep flying!

In the middle of the Gulf, I saw something that I had never even heard of before. It was a huge fish that seemed to be sunning itself near the surface of the water. From that distance, it seemed to be on its side. It had two large fins that stuck out very far toward the back of the top and bottom of its body, kind of like a massive turtle turned on its side with only its two rear legs, but instead of shell, the whole body was flesh, and it appeared that the entire back portion of the body was a sort of non-protruding tail that wagged lazily back and forth. As it lay on its side, a couple of sea gulls stood on it and appeared as if they were eating something. I learned later that it was called a Gulf Sunfish, or Mola-Mola. I would never forget the sight.

As the big eye of the sun descended into the deep blue sea, the flock altered course to the west, and I knew that I must leave them. This time the dusk didn't bring anything on the horizon to land on, so I continued to fly, alone. The stars came out one by one, and with no lights around from human cities, they brilliantly lit up the sky. I could tell the constellations clearly, and in addition to the instinct that was guiding me, saw that I was right on course by the North Star, the last one in the Little Dipper's handle. It was good to have that assurance. I had seen clear nights before, but nothing ever like this. Over and over a falling star would come down so far that I was sure I could reach out and catch it. After several hours of flying, I saw lights on the horizon, not of fishing boats or big ships, but lights from houses and businesses. They flickered for a long while, but as I ascended a little for a better look there was no denying it; land was before me!

I descended, and since it was the middle of the night, I decided to get some sleep. I found our hummingbird feeder and had some much needed nectar, ate some mosquitoes, and retreated to the familiar grove of trees for some much needed rest. I slept past sunrise for the first time since I had become a hummingbird, and went straight to the feeders. After a long, long, drink I flew all around the house looking for Grandpa. I was ready to change back. I thought it through, what were the rules? I had to go back to the same exact place, and I assumed I could change back as I had on the beach almost four months earlier. Four months! How was all of this going to work? I was really going to get it for being gone so long. And no one was going to believe my story.

After tapping just hard enough on the glass that was now on my Grandpa's porch for the wintertime, I was able to get his attention while he was reading the paper with his morning cup of coffee. He noticed me, and came out to the porch. I flew right up to him and placed my binocular shaped red mark directly in front of him. He laughed a hearty laugh and took out his cell phone again. Pressing no buttons, he put it up to his ear and spoke.

"So, my little friend, you've made it back!" he said. "I was hoping I'd see you soon. But what's this?" He pointed to my band. My band! I had forgotten all about it. Could I change back with it on? I didn't like the idea of going through life as a peg leg if it cut off circulation when I changed.

"That belongs to the U. S. Geological Survey," Grandpa said calmly. "They will want it back. I've got a friend who works for them and will want to know about this. I'll ask him to come and take it off, since I'm not sure how to do it, and don't want to risk hurting you. Is that all right with you?" I bobbed up and down excitedly. He held out his finger, and I landed gingerly on it. He set me down on the perch of one of the feeders and told me that he needed to make a call. I drank more nectar, thankful that Grandpa was such a help.

The man arrived a few hours later, and I flew to Grandpa's hand and perched once more. The man seemed surprised that I was so tame, but Grandpa told him that this feeder was my territory, and that I came there a lot. He took me in his other hand just as the scientist had before, and began working on my banded leg. It didn't take long, and I hardly felt anything at all. Pretty soon, he held up the hollow ring in his hand. Grandpa said, "Would you mind if once you get the information that you need, I go ahead and keep this? It would mean a lot to me." The man said that it was first and foremost to be used for scientific observation, but that it would make a nice souvenir. Once he was gone, Grandpa came to me and said, "Now, once you have built back your body weight some, return to the place where you started. Take whatever time you need."

But I was ready to change back *now*! I didn't want to wait a few days or a week to build back my body weight. Enough time had passed already. But, once again, Grandpa had never steered me wrong before, so over the next few agonizing days I built back my body weight to almost where it had been before. It was time.

I flew back like a shot to the place where it all started, and even found the flower bushes where I had seen the hummingbird drinking, and took a long last drink of sweet nectar. It wasn't quite as tasty as what I had found in Costa Rica, but it was good, and I wanted to savor it. I landed, standing in the precise spot where I had first discovered myself as a bird and been filmed by Ned. There was no one around. Gently, I bowed my head forward and touched my long bill to my chest.

My neck burned where the shape of the Binoculars was, and soon a bright light began to shine from it. The feathers became shafts once again and eventually turned back into small hairs. My arms shifted around my shoulders, coming down and forward, and hands grew out of what had been wings for months. My legs grew longer and longer, and I shot up vertically standing up so quickly that I lost my balance and fell over. My heart slowed down so that it seemed to be beating just a little above what I remembered was torpor, and my body temperature lowered a few degrees. Pretty soon there I was, an ordinary boy named Ben, just lying in the pine needles, wearing the same clothes I had worn that fateful day when it all began.

I was alone, and extremely thirsty. I opened my mouth to speak, but could hardly make a sound. I remembered that there was water nearby in the swamp, and scrambled toward it not caring if it was sanitary or not. I ducked down to get some from the swamp.

"I wouldn't do that if I were you. You could get E Coli that way. And what would your Mother say to me if I let you drink out of the swamp? Here, I brought some that's better." I looked up and saw Grandpa sitting calmly on the bench at the overlook! I clapped my hands excitedly, still unable to speak, ran to him and gave him a great big hug. He held out a bottle of water to me, and I downed the entire bottle.

I stared at him in disbelief. He said, "Your family will be here soon. Follow my lead." I just nodded. I was too stunned to do much else. At that moment, my entire family came around along the path, and Grandpa calmly walked towards them. I followed. They all looked exactly as they did four months ago, they were even wearing the same clothes!

"Just where have you been? We've been worried sick about you!" my Mom said.

"Ben, you remember that we all agreed to meet back at the parking area at 5:00 PM, right? Where have you been all of this time?" Dad asked, restating Mom's question.

I opened my mouth to speak, but Grandpa spoke right up and cut me off. "He was with me. I'm sorry I didn't tell you about it. There was a special bird watching project we needed to do together," he said. Grandpa looked back at me and winked.

"Well, all right, but next time, please let us know. It's not like Ben to be *an hour* late!" Dad said.

An hour! What were they talking about an hour? I looked at my watch, and it was 6 PM on the same day I had left! I began to open my mouth, and Grandpa shot me a stern look and raised his index finger to his lips warning me to be quiet. My eyes got wide, and I just looked down.

"Well, whatever happened, I'm glad you're all right. That's what matters the most!" Mom said, hugging me tightly. She then held my shoulders away from her and looked me over thoroughly and said, "Honey, are you feeling all right? You've lost some weight, and have a lot more muscle!"

"He's been running the sands here on the island the last couple of days. It does wonders for your metabolism!" Grandpa said. I smiled and nodded enthusiastically. She looked at him skeptically. Grandpa smiled, too, and said, "Now, I'm sure that we're all a bit hungry after this long day. Let's go home. Grandma will have dinner ready."

We all headed back toward the car, and Ned came up to me, annoying as ever. "Hey, where were you? I never saw you after we went to the swamp. I got some great shots with my new camera!" he said. "I can't wait to post them online! Hey, did you ever get to see anything out of those worthless binoculars?" I just nodded, and told him I couldn't wait to see his pictures. I knew that one was of me learning to fly as a hummingbird, but I knew for sure I couldn't tell *him* that.

We arrived back home, and Grandma had a great big meal on the table for all of us, complete with mashed potatoes, corn bread, beans, and *fried chicken*. I looked over all of the good food, and hungry as I was, just couldn't bring myself to eat a bird. Once I sat down, however, I noticed a gnat on the table, and before I could stop myself I grabbed it and put it in my mouth and swallowed it. Somehow, it didn't taste as good now that I was a person again. When I looked up, Ned was watching me, and I just said, "Extra protein," and nodded my head, smiling. He just slowly nodded his head with a confused look. I chowed down on everything else, eating three full plates, and added more sugar to my lemonade to make it extra sweet. I knew that my life would never be the same. Mom wanted to know if I was all right. She had never seen me eat so much.

XV. The Key

The next morning, Grandpa got me up early, we had some breakfast and got in his car. Once there, he asked me, "How long were you gone?"

"Four months. How is it possible that I was only gone an hour?" I asked.

"Now, think back. What time was it when you first changed into a hummingbird?" Grandpa asked. He was right. I had changed after about 45 minutes on the trail, and that would mean that it was about 2 PM.

"Two o'clock," I said.

"That's what I thought. Were there any other markings on your Binoculars when you changed? Think hard," Grandpa said.

I thought about it, and then remembered the "30:1" I had seen in the eyepiece each time I had changed. I told Grandpa about it.

"Thirty, colon, one," he said slowly and thoughtfully. I nodded. What did it mean?

There was silence for a moment, and then he laughed. "I've got it!" he said. "The first column must be days, and the second must be hours. Think about it. You were gone 120 days, and when you returned, only four hours had passed. So that's how Graham used to do it! There's got to be other settings, too, because sometimes he would go all the way to the southern tip of South America according to the map at his house, and I don't ever remember him being gone for long at all. As far as most people on the island knew, he was here all of the time." I held up the Binoculars, and looked into the lens. I saw the "30:1" clearly, and then began to play around with the lenses. The eyepiece on the lens that was like a spyglass turned, and there was a little wheel inside. I turned the lens one click, and looked into the binoculars again. Clear as could be, it now read:

60:1

I continued turning it and found all sorts of settings ranging from 1:1 going as high as

365:1. I couldn't believe it!

"You mean that I could be gone 365 days, *a full year*, and only one hour would pass?" I asked.

"It looks like it," Grandpa said. Now I was *really* glad to have someone else in on the secret.

"Well, here we are at our destination," Grandpa said. He had pulled into the driveway of Ol' Salt's house and parked around the back. We got out of the car, walked up to the back door, and he got out his key. The key turned in the lock, but the door stuck hard. It took both of us bumping it with our shoulders to open the door, and we both went inside.

"I want you to mark your journey on the map," he said.

I looked the Map over with new wonder. Seeing all of these journeys, tears of understanding welled up in my eyes. I was part of a tradition that had gone back hundreds of years, and had remained a secret to all but a select few. Grandpa handed me a very old looking Calligraphy type pen, and I got some paper to practice with it before I marked my path on The Map. Strangely, the pen had black ink when I dipped it into the ink well and practiced on the paper, but when I began marking my path on the Map, the ink turned an iridescent green, the same exact color I had been as a bird. I marked the spot where I had turned back to a boy and caught the lobsters and fish, and the ultimate destination in Costa Rica. I saw all of the other lines and wondered about those journeys. How long had the owner taken on each of them? Did it really take such little time out of their life? I held my Binoculars out, looking at them, and remarked to my Grandpa what a powerful tool they were.

"Yes, they are," he said. "I'm glad they are in your hands. Ol' Salt couldn't have picked a better person." I blushed in embarrassment and looked at the ground.

"So how old is he, *really*, then?" I asked.

"I don't rightly know." Grandpa said. "There's no telling how many trips he took with those, but enough to give him some bird like habits. Didn't you notice?" I nodded. "Now, this place is going to take some real cleaning up and a little bit of fixing up," Grandpa said. "Would you like to help me?" Grandpa asked.

"I'd love to!" I said, excited at the opportunity to help Grandpa on a project that might unlock the answers to more questions that I had.

Somehow, I thought I had just scratched the surface of learning about the Binoculars.

"Great!" Grandpa said. "We'll start right now."

We began with the unpleasant task of taking out the garbage. About nine o'clock, Grandpa called my family and let them know that I was helping him with a project, and we worked up until lunch time getting garbage out to the curb. It was far from the excitement I had hoped for. The house was really big, and each room had to be cleaned up. We went home for lunch and had fish and chips.

Ned wanted to come with us after lunch along with Beth, and so we all went to the house and began working with the garbage. At the end of the day, it looked a lot better as there was no garbage around, but there was still clutter everywhere. Ned was thoroughly disgusted, and Beth didn't want to come back ever again. I couldn't blame them. If not for the journey I had just taken, I would have felt the same way.

We got back to the house for dinner, ate, played games at the house, and I went for a walk on the beach to see the stars. Of course, Ned tagged along, and began to nag me with questions.

"Did you see anything interesting while you were gone today?" he asked.

"A few things," I replied in an understated tone, not wanting to let him in on anything.

"Did you see anything interesting?" I asked.

"Yes. I had an interesting experience today while you were gone. I found a hummingbird, and helped him learn to fly," he said.

"People don't teach hummingbirds to fly, they learn from their mothers," I said uneasily.

"No. I mean, there was something different about this bird. Its eyes were really bright, like it understood me when I talked," Ned said. I was really starting to get worried that he may have seen me change, but decided not to show it.

"Really? And you say that I'm strange sometimes," I said, trying to cover.

"Yeah. Ya' know, at first when I saw it, I thought about just kicking it away," he said, his voice like I had always known it, and then he continued in a more calm and caring way, "But then when I saw how helpless it was there, I just wanted to do something for it." I was beginning to feel better.

"What did you do?" I asked.

"I held it in my hand, and it was amazingly tame. I didn't know what to do, but it chattered to me and pointed its head toward some flowers," he said.

"Really?" I said.

"Yeah. I was really worried about dropping him, but he sort of directed me to the flowers and began to drink and drink. After that, he flew away. It was the most amazing experience I have ever had, face to face with such a fragile, beautiful thing."

"There's more to you than you let on. Deep down, there's a decent person in there," I said.

"Yeah, there is. Just don't let anybody else know or I'll pound you!" Ned said resuming his former tone.

"Now, that's the Ned I know!" I said, teasing him.

"Why were you willing to get the trash out of that old coot's house?" he asked, changing the subject. It was an annoying comment, and I took it to heart more than I should have.

"Ol' Salt was a great man," I said seriously. "I don't expect you to understand."

"You're acting weird," said Ned. "Are you feeling O.K.?"

"I've never been better," I said more calmly, looking up at the little dipper. It meant more to me now than it ever had before.

"What are you staring at?" Ned asked.

"If you are quiet and just take some time and look up at the stars, you'll find that you are different. A peace comes over you that's hard to explain, kind of like you felt with that bird," I said.

At that, we both sat down listening to the waves crashing on the shore, and looking up at the perfectly clear night sky. Every now and then a star would fall, and we would both ooh and ahh and silently make our own wishes on the shooting star. Other than that, neither of us spoke at all. It was in these moments that I learned that when you struggle with someone, sometimes just doing something with them *not speaking* brings you closer to an understanding of them. I didn't have nearly as much trouble with Ned after that, and we began to become much closer once I began to look at him as a person instead of an annoyance. My Dad would be proud.

For the first time in my life, I felt like I was thinking more like a person who was at least trying to grow up. I think it would have taken me much longer if it weren't for my trips as a bird and the longing I had to fit in as something that was truly out of place: a boy trying to be a bird. Now, it was time to adjust back into life as a human being in my own culture, which was more of a shock than I had expected. I didn't crave the same foods anymore, and my sense of time was confused at the moment. I looked at the world with a newly found respect that I hadn't had before.

Later when we went back to the house Ned showed me the video that he had taken in the bird sanctuary. I was kind of embarrassed when it got to the part about me trying to stand up, but I saw something that made me take notice. Not only did I have the binoculars-shaped mark on my throat, but also ever so slightly in yellow on my back was the same shaped marking. I had never seen my back the whole time that I was a bird, and had just assumed that it was a straight green like most of the other Ruby-Throats I had seen. Maybe that's how the hawk on the shore of the Yucatan recognized me on my return flight.

The next day, Grandpa took me to Ol' Salt's house and we cleaned it up some more. Ned and Beth didn't want to come, so it took longer. We organized a lot of his old stuff, and when it was time to fix some things, I asked Grandpa to leave the boards in the attic off, just so that I would always have a place to come. I knew then that I could take long trips in the night, and knew also that I would need a place to land and sleep if I returned too late. We went into the basement and cleaned it up, and I thought that it would be a great place to hide something dug into the sandy earth, so I dug for a while down there but didn't find anything of interest. After getting it into pretty good order, we left the house.

That night everyone was watching a movie in the living room, and I decided to go to bed early. Besides, you could hardly hear the movie for the obnoxiously loud ray gun that Ned was playing with, oblivious to the fact that everyone else wanted to watch. He was still the same old Ned. I was still tired from the long flight a few days before, and slipped out of the room unnoticed. Before going to bed, however, I wanted to look over my Binoculars again. I took them out of their old case marked GAK, unwrapped them from their tattered cloth as I had before, admiring the list of initials that now included mine:

J-B M B
R F
E P G
R S
B M B
G A K
B W A

I sat staring at the initials, wondering who these people were, and if finding out and learning about their lives would unlock more mysteries behind this wondrous artifact. As I sat and wondered, I drifted off to sleep, not even noticing the din of the TV in the room below.

Epilogue: What I Learned After the Trip

We had a great time the rest of that week. Each day, Grandpa and I would go to Ol' Salt's house early before the rest of the family was awake and do a little something to fix up the place. It was hard work, but worth it in the end just to spend some time with Grandpa and learn a little bit more about Ol' Salt. Grandpa said that I was "learning the importance of hard work and a job well done." I just liked to help, and was still wondering what was ahead for me as I looked through the belongings of the previous owner of the Binoculars. Ned and I got along a lot better, I saw that he could actually be a decent person, and became more patient with him than I had been in the past. He appreciated it, and we did a lot of things together.

After my journey was over, I spent as much time as possible looking things up in books or online about my adventures. Grandpa and Grandma had a small room that they called "The Library", and I spent a lot of time in there with their books on birds and geography. There was so much that I wanted to know and learn. I wished that I had been able to learn this stuff before my trip, but it wasn't like I could have planned on turning into a hummingbird and migrating south to Costa Rica. Here is a little bit of what I found.

On Hummingbirds: There are over 340 known species of hummingbirds, curiously only in North and South America, no other continents. They range from as far north as Alaska to the southern tip of Argentina. The Ruby-Throated Hummingbird lives most of its life in the Eastern portion of the United States and Canada, and migrates each year to Central America, mainly to the Western Coast but some live in Mexico, Honduras, and Nicaragua. Just as I discovered in my time as one, most of them fly 500 miles over the Gulf of Mexico non-stop, although some may be able to find rest spots along the way like I did on ships or other places. Some believe that they travel alone as I did on the way, and some believe that they travel in disparate flocks made up of different types of non-predatory songbirds as I did on my return flight.

All hummingbirds beat their wings extremely fast, from as little as 50 times per second to as much as 200 times per second during a dive. There are hummingbirds that are very similar to the Ruby-Throated Hummingbirds in the Western parts of the United States and Canada called the Anna's Hummingbirds in which the male's entire head is red, not just the throat. There are also three other types that live west of the Mississippi River called the Rufous, Allen's, and Costa's Hummingbirds. These range from all the way up into Canada and Alaska down into Mexico and Central America during migration, and so take a similar journey as

I did. The difference is that they are able to stay over land when on their migration path.

On Preening: All that I knew about preening I learned from watching other birds, and as my feathers began to become dry and not quite as waterproof, I gathered oil from the furthest point on my back (the preen gland) and spread it evenly among my feathers.

On Stingrays: Stingrays are common in the Gulf of Mexico. They only use their stingers for self defense, so we learned when we were very young to scuffle our feet in the sand which keeps you from accidentally stepping on one. If you do that, they will simply swim away, as they are not aggressive creatures. The Golden or Cow-Nosed Rays migrate in large schools of as many as ten thousand in a clockwise direction from the Northern Gulf Coast toward the Yucatan Peninsula. Other types of stingrays do not migrate at all, remaining year round in their locales.

On Orcas: Killer Whales have been discovered in all oceans of the world, from the arctic to the tropical waters of the Gulf of Mexico. There have been many sightings of these whales in the Gulf since 1993. They are of a species that usually stays in deep water over 600 feet, and travel in large pods (or families) of 30-60, although there have been reported instances of 75 in a pod. As many as four large pods have been seen traveling closely together in the Gulf totaling over 200 whales in one area at a time. It is believed that there are around 500 killer whales living in the Gulf of Mexico.

The sounds I heard as I encountered them must have been their echolocation, or sonar. They use a sonar system that is more highly advanced than any that man has made, using a combination of high frequency pitches made with their nostrils which they use for communication with each other, and a rapid series of clicking sounds used for navigation and location of prey.

On "Weed Lines" or Sargassum grass: Sargassum grass is a saltwater floating plant that grows clusters of small round grape-sized bladders that are filled with a gas that causes the whole plant to float. Sometimes they are just these plants, but often an ecosystem develops below them, resulting in the place that I found to rest. They can grow so long that they can be seen from outer space by satellite images. In the Atlantic Ocean, large amounts of it all come together in what is known as the Great Sargasso Sea, because the ocean currents flow around the sea's center. It is here in the heart of the famous Bermuda Triangle where no trade winds blow, that a huge section of Sargassum covers an area almost two-thirds the size of the continental United States. Columbus wrote about it in the notes of his voyages. While nothing this large exists in the Gulf of Mexico, it still creates large areas where debris gets caught and birds can find rest.

On Gulf Dolphin (Mahi-Mahi): Not to be confused with the bottle-nosed dolphin, a mammal that breathes air, the Gulf Dolphin is a beautiful fish also known as the Mahi-Mahi. They are highly sought after both as trophy fish as well as for food. They have a long deep blue dorsal fin that runs from the head down the entire length of their golden body to the tail, and are often found harboring under a line of sargassum grass. Deeper down under the sargassum, the longer, thinner fish I mentioned was the Wahoo, coveted by sport fisherman.

On Rock Lobster: Also known as Spiny Lobster or Caribbean Lobster, these creatures live in the Southern Atlantic Ocean, Caribbean Sea, and the southern parts of the Gulf of Mexico. Many of the lobster tails sold at restaurants in America are actually Rock Lobster Tails. Another variety is found in the subtropical and tropical waters of the Pacific Ocean.

On Chichen Itza and the Equinox: I learned a lot from the tour guide, but it wasn't until I got back that I found a video online of what happens twice a year at the equinox. On a clear day, the sun shows a very clear image of a serpent all the way down the outside banister of the pyramid's staircase, the head of which is carved at the bottom of the banister. The entire city is a mystery, for no one knows why the beautiful and large cities of Central America were abandoned all about the same time.

On Monkeys in Central America: I had always thought of monkeys as African, but there are several types in Central America; Howler Monkeys, Red-face Monkeys, and White-face Monkeys all make their homes in the rain forests of Central America.

On Mola Mola Sunfish: The world's largest bony fish, these remarkable creatures live in many tropical and temperate oceans of the world, including the Gulf of Mexico. Mola in Latin means "millstone", referring to the rounded shape of the fish. They travel very close to the surface, sunning and eating zooplankton, occasionally jumping out of the water to get rid of parasites. Young fish of this type are around 450 pounds, and as they mature they can grow up to 5000 pounds.

The Binoculars have changed my life dramatically just in the last few weeks. They have helped me fulfill a dream of travel, grow up a little bit faster, and have succeeded in making me a better learner. I can't wait to see what the future holds! But even without them, I have discovered that I am able to go all over by reading books and going online for research. I still want to learn all that I can about the world in which I live, and now have an incredible tool to do just that. I plan on helping my mother with her gardens when we go back home so that we will have a section specifically for hummingbirds.

I was back at home when the email arrived about two and a half weeks later with a picture of me with Pedro, Enrique, and José on the top of Chichen Itza. I printed it out, and although the only one I ever showed it to was Grandpa, it will always be one of my most treasured possessions. Every now and then, something will slip out that I learned from that trip and if anyone ever asks me how I know that, I just smile and say, "A little bird told me."

Bibliography

Wild Bird Guides: Ruby-throated Hummingbird. Robert Sargent, 1999, Stackpole Books, Mechanicsburg, Pennsylvania.

The World of the Hummingbird. Robert Burton, 2001, Firefly Books, Buffalo, New York.

Peterson Field Guides: Hummingbirds of North America. Sheri L. Williamson, 2001, Houghton Mifflin Co. New York, New York.

Enjoying Hummingbirds In the Wild & In Your Yard. Larry & Terrie Gates, 2008, Stackpole Books, Mechanicsburg, PA.

http://www.hummingbirdsplus.org

http://www.learner.org/jnorth/humm/index.html

http://www.worldofhummingbirds.com/types.php

http://www.orcafree.org/how.html

http://www.wkrg.com/alabama/article/killer_whales_in_the_gulf_of_mexico/21653/Dec-05-2008_6-33-pm/

http://www.bermuda-triangle.org/html/sargasso_sea.html

http://marinebio.org/species.asp?id=155

Brief Excerpt from Book Two

Later that week after my amazing adventures as a hummingbird, Ned and his family left on a day trip to some nearby gardens. I had hidden my Binoculars under the bed in our room, and now that I didn't have to worry about him seeing, I wanted to look them over again. I carefully removed them from the sturdy old leather case, gingerly unwrapped the delicate cloth from them, and heard a clinking sound as I dropped the old wrapping of my Binoculars on the bed. I picked up the cloth again, and noticed a small pocket that had been hurriedly sewn into it. I got out my knife and carefully cut the stitching with the little scissors it had on it. Two small keys fell out, an old skeleton key and a more modern key.

There were no markings on either of the keys as I held them up to the light. They simply appeared to be plain. I searched around in the case for anything else I may have overlooked until now, but found nothing else of interest. I wondered what they were to. Knowing that I couldn't tackle this tonight, I carefully put them away and drifted off to sleep. I went with Grandpa and looked for something that these keys might fit into, but found nothing. I decided not to take another trip until I had planned things out more the next time, but I was sure that another adventure had just begun…

About the Author

Ben's Binoculars was inspired by my love of travel and fascination with all of creation. All my life I have been a part of a family that travels. I moved from the West Coast of the United States to South America at the age of five years old, and was deeply affected by the culture and people as well as the beauty of the jungles, mountains, and waterfalls there.

Later in my life I lived on the East Coast and the Deep South in the United States before going to college in Southern Appalachia. In college, I spent time living in Europe, learning more about life in different parts of the world.

Later I married and began teaching elementary, middle, and high school before becoming a full-time college professor in the Midwest of the United States. Over the past decade, my family has traveled to the Gulf Coast many times, where we fell in love with the beauty and warmth of both the climate and the people. My wife and I decided to settle on the Alabama Gulf Coast in the last few years, and we find it a fascinating and wondrous place to raise our two children.